'HERMANN HESSE IS A GREAT WRITER IN PRECISELY THE MODERN SENSE'
The New York Times

Hesse was born in Germany in 1877. During the first world war, and as his protest against German militarism, he went to live in Switzerland where he died in 1962, shortly after his eighty-fifth birthday.

He started to write and publish poetry when he was twenty-one, published his first novel, *Peter Camenzind*, when he was twenty-six; then followed over the years such masterpieces as *Demian*, *Siddhartha*, and *Steppenwolf* among others. In 1946 he received the Nobel Prize for Literature. Although Hesse's novels mirror the chaotic years of the first world war and its aftermath they today, half a century later, read as freshly as the day they were first published – which is a sad comment on the last fifty years of human history. His influence on today's disenchanted youth is easy to understand, they are discovering in him a fellow-traveller who, like them, passionately hates war and the dehumanisation that wars bring with them. Like them, too, he understands the deep human need for a private morality. He shares with them the hopes of a happier future. And he has nothing but contempt for the shabby morality of the bourgeoisie. In brief, Hesse's world of outcasts of one kind or another – the world of drop-outs, 'freaks', 'hippies' of fifty years ago – is immensely meaningful to 1970's young people. And his hopeful belief that the outcasts he depicts, while in the process of losing themselves are also on the way to finding themselves, is bracing indeed. We shall hear much more of Hermann Hesse.

Also by Hermann Hesse in Panther Books

Demian

Hermann Hesse

The Journey to the East

translated by Hilda Rosner

Introductory chapter by Timothy Leary

Panther

Granada Publishing Limited
Special overseas edition first published in 1972 by
Panther Books Ltd
Frogmore, St Albans, Herts AL2 2NF
Reprinted 1972, 1973

First published in Great Britain by Peter Owen
Limited 1956. Reprinted twice
Copyright © Hermann Hesse 1956
Translation copyright © Peter Owen 1956
Revised translation copyright © Peter Owen 1964
Introductory chapter 'Poet of the Interior Journey' by
Timothy Leary copyright © The League for
Spiritual Discovery Inc. 1966
Made and printed in Great Britain by
C. Nicholls & Company Ltd
The Philips Park Press, Manchester
Set in Monotype Garamond

Poet of the Interior Journey

Poet of the Interior Journey*

by *Timothy Leary*

Hermann Hesse was born in July 1877 in the little Swabian town of Calw, the son of Protestant missionaries. His home background and education were pietistic, intellectual, classical. He entered a theological seminary at the age of fourteen with the intention of taking orders and left two years later. In Basle he learned the book trade and made his living as a bookseller and editor of classical German literary texts. He became acquainted with Jacob Burckhardt, the great Swiss historian and philosopher, who later served as the model for the portrait of Father Jacobus in *The Bead Game*. In 1914 Hesse's 'unpatriotic' anti-war attitude brought him official censure and newspaper attacks. Two months after the outbreak of the war, an essay entitled 'O Freunde, nicht diese Töne' ('O Friends, not these tones') was published in the *Neue Zürcher Zeitung*; it was an appeal to the youth of Germany, deploring the stampede to disaster.

In 1911 he travelled in India. From 1914 to 1919 he lived in Berne, working in the German embassy as an assistant

*Reprinted from *Psychedelic Review,* No. 3. This paper was co-authored by Ralph Metzner, editor of the *Review.* It has also appeared in *The Politics of Ecstasy* by Timothy Leary (Paladin, 1970).

for prisoners of war. A series of personal crises accompanied the external crisis of the war: his father died; his youngest son fell seriously ill; his wife suffered a nervous breakdown and was hospitalized. In 1919, the year of the publication of *Demian*, he moved to the small village of Montagnola by the Lake of Lugano and remained there till the end of his life. In 1923 he acquired Swiss citizenship and in 1927 remarried. Hesse steeped himself in Indian and Chinese literature and philosophy, the latter particularly through the masterful translations of Chinese texts by Richard Wilhelm. In 1931 he remarried a third time and moved to another house in Montagnola which had been provided for him by his friend H. C. Bodmer. In 1946 he was awarded the Nobel Prize; in 1962, at the age of eighty-five, he died. Asked once what were the most important influences in his life, he said they were 'the Christian and completely non-nationalist spirit of my parents' home', the 'reading of the great Chinese masters', and the figure of the historian Jacob Burckhardt.

Few writers have chronicled with such dispassionate lucidity and fearless honesty the progress of the soul through the states of life. *Peter Camenzind* (1904), *Demian** (1919), *Siddhartha* (1922), *Steppenwolf* (1927), *Narziss und Goldmund* (1930), *Journey to the East* (1932), *Magister Ludi* (1943) – different versions of spiritual autobiography, different maps of the interior path. Each new step revises the picture of all the previous steps; each experience opens up new worlds of discovery in a constant effort to communicate the vision.

*Also available in Panther Books.

As John Cage is fond of reminding us, writing is one thing and reading is another. All writings, all authors are thoroughly misunderstood. Most wise men do not write because they know this. The wise man has penetrated through the verbal curtain, seen and known and felt the life process. We owe him our gratitude when he remains with us and tries to induce us to share the joy.

The great writer is the wise man who feels compelled to translate the message into words. The message is, of course, around us and in us at all moments. Everything is a clue. Everything contains all the message. To pass it on in symbols is unnecessary but perhaps the greatest performance of man.

Wise men write (with deliberation) in the esoteric. It's the way of making a rose or a baby. The exoteric form is maya, the hallucinatory façade. The meaning is within. The greatness of a great book lies in the esoteric, the seed meaning concealed behind the net of symbols. All great writers write the same book, changing only the exoteric trappings of their time and tribe.

Hermann Hesse is one of the great writers of our time. He wrote Finnegan's Wake in several German versions. In addition to being a wise man, he could manipulate words well enough to win the Nobel Prize.

Most readers miss the message of Hesse. Entranced by the pretty dance of plot and theme, they overlook the seed message. Hesse is a trickster. Like nature in April, he dresses up his code in fancy plumage. The literary reader picks the fruit, eats quickly, and tosses the core to the ground. But the seed, the electrical message, the code, is in the core.

Take *Siddhartha*[1] – the primer for young bodhisattvas, written when Hesse was forty-five. Watch the old magician warming up to his work. We are introduced to a proud young man, strong, handsome, supple-limbed, graceful. Siddhartha is young and ambitious. He seeks to attain the greatest prize of all – enlightenment. Cosmic one-up-manship. He masters each of the otherworldly games. The Vedas. Asceticism. Matches his wits against the Buddha himself. Tantric worldly success. 'We find consolations, we learn tricks with which we deceive ourselves, but the essential thing – the way – we do not find.' 'Wisdom is not communicable.' 'I can love a stone, Govinda, and a tree or a piece of bark. These are things and one can love things. But one cannot love words . . . Nirvana is not a thing; there is only the word Nirvana.' Then in the last pages of the book, Hermann Hesse, Nobel Prize novelist, uses words to describe the wonderful illumination of Govinda, who

> no longer saw the face of his friend Siddhartha. Instead he saw other faces, many faces, a long series, a continuous stream of faces – hundreds, thousands, which all came and disappeared and yet all seemed to be there at the same time, which all continually changed and renewed themselves and which were yet all Siddhartha. He saw the face of a fish, of a carp, with tremendous painfully opened mouth, a dying fish with dimmed eyes. He saw the face of a newly born child, red and full of wrinkles, ready to cry. He saw the face of a murderer, saw him plunge a knife into the body of a man; at the same moment he saw this criminal kneeling down, bound, and his head cut off by an executioner. He saw the naked

bodies of men and women in the postures and transports of passionate love. He saw corpses stretched out, still, cold, empty. He saw the heads of animals, boars, crocodiles, elephants, oxen, birds. He saw Krishna and Agni. He saw all these forms and faces in a thousand relationships to each other, all helping each other, loving, hating and destroying each other and become newly born. Each one was mortal, a passionate, painful example of all that is transitory. Yet none of them died, they only changed, were always reborn, continually had a new face: only time stood between one face and another. And all these forms and faces rested, flowed, reproduced, swam past and merged into each other, and over them all there was continually something thin, unreal and yet existing, stretched across like thin glass or ice, like a transparent skin, shell, form or mask of water – and this mask was Siddhartha's smiling face which Govinda touched with his lips at that moment. And Govinda saw that this mask-like smile, this smile of unity over the flowing forms, this smile of simultaneousness over the thousands of births and deaths – this smile of Siddhartha – was exactly the same as the calm, delicate, impenetrable, perhaps gracious, perhaps mocking, wise, thousand-fold smile of Gotama, the Buddha, as he had perceived it with awe a hundred times. It was in such a manner, Govinda knew, that the Perfect One smiled.

Those who have taken one of the psychedelic drugs may recognize

Govinda's vision as a classic LSD sequence. The direct visual confrontation with the unity of all men, the unity of life. That Hesse can write words such as unity, love, Nirvana *is easily understood. Every Hindu textbook gives you the jargon. But his description of the visual details of the cosmic vision, the retinal specifics, is more impressive. Whence came to Hesse these concrete sensations? The similarity to the consciousness-expanding drug experience is startling. The specific, concrete 'is-ness' of the illuminated moment usually escapes the abstract philosopher of mysticism. Did Hesse reach this visionary state himself? By meditation? Spontaneously? Did H.H., the novelist himself, use the chemical path to enlightenment?*

The answer to these questions is suggested in the next lesson of the master: *Steppenwolf*[2] – a novel of crisis, pain, conflict, torture – at least on the surface. Hesse writes in a letter: 'If my life were not a dangerous painful experiment, if I did not constantly skirt the abyss and feel the void under my feet, my life would have no meaning and I would not have been able to write anything.' Most readers sophisticated in psychodynamics recognize the drama presented – the conflict between ego and id, between spirit and material civilization, the 'wolfish, satanic instincts that lurk within even our civilized selves', as the jacket of the paperback edition has it. 'These readers [writes Hesse] have completely overlooked that above the Steppenwolf and his problematical life there exists a second, higher, timeless world . . . which contrasts the suffering of the Steppenwolf with a transpersonal and transtemporal world of faith, that the book certainly tells of pain and suffering but is the story of a believer not a tale of despair.'

As in *Siddhartha,* Hesse involves the reader in his fantastic tale, his ideas, his mental acrobatics, only to show at the end that the whole structure is illusory mind play. The mental rug is suddenly pulled out from under the gullible psychodynamic reader. This Zen trick is evident on at least two levels in the *Steppenwolf.* First, in the little 'Treatise', a brilliant portrait of Harry, the man with two souls: the man – refined, clever, and interesting; and the wolf – savage, untameable, dangerous, and strong. The treatise describes his swings of mood, his bursts of creativity, his ambivalent relationship to the bourgeoisie, his fascination with suicide, his inability to reconcile the two conflicting selves. A breathtakingly subtle psychological analysis. Then, the sleight of hand:

> There is . . . a fundamental delusion to make clear. All interpretation, all psychology, all attempts to make things comprehensible, require the medium of theories, mythologies and lies; and a self-respecting author should . . . dissipate these lies so far as may be in his power. . . . Harry consists of a hundred or a thousand selves, not of two. His life oscillates, as everyone's does, not merely between two poles, such as the body and the spirit, the saint and the sinner, but between thousands...
> Man is an onion made up of a hundred integuments, a texture made up of many threads. The ancient Asiatics knew this well enough, and in the Buddhist

Yoga an exact technique was devised for unmasking the illusion of the personality. The human merry-go-round sees many changes: the illusion that cost India the efforts of thousands of years to unmask is the same illusion that the West has laboured just as hard to maintain and strengthen.

The dualistic self-image is described – the fascinating and compelling Freudian metaphor – and is then exposed as a delusion, a limited, pitiful perspective, a mind game. The second example of this trick occurs at the end of the book. We have followed Hesse in his descriptions of Harry as he runs through a series of vain attempts to conquer his despair – through alcohol, through sex, through music, through friendship with the exotic musician Pablo; finally he enters the Magic Theatre. 'Price of Admission, your Mind'. In other words, a mind-loss experience.

> From a recess in the wall [Pablo] took three glasses and a quaint little bottle. . . . He filled the three glasses from the bottle and taking three long thin yellow cigarettes from the box and a box of matches from the pocket of his silk jacket he gave us a light. . . . Its effect was immeasurably enlivening and delightful – as though one were filled with gas and had no longer any gravity.

Pablo says

> You were striving, were you not, for escape? You have a longing to forsake this world and its reality and

to penetrate to a reality more native to you, to a world beyond time. ... You know, of course, where this other world lies hidden. It is the world of your own soul that you seek. Only within yourself exists that other reality for which you long. ... All I can give you is the opportunity, the impulse, the key. I help you to make your own world visible. ... This ... theatre has as many doors into as many boxes as you please, ten or a hundred or a thousand, and behind each door exactly what you seek awaits you. ... You have no doubt guessed long since that the conquest of time and the escape from reality, or however else it may be that you choose to describe your longing, means simply the wish to be relieved of your so-called personality. That is the prison where you lie. And if you enter the theatre as you are, you would see everything through the eyes of Harry and the old spectacles of the Steppenwolf. You are therefore requested to lay these spectacles aside and to be so kind as to leave your highly esteemed personality here in the cloak-room, where you will find it again when you wish. The pleasant dance from which you have just come, the treatise on the Steppenwolf, and the little stimulant that we have only this moment partaken of may have sufficiently prepared you.

It seems clear that Hesse is describing a psychedelic experience, a drug-induced loss of self, a journey to the inner world. Each door in the Magic Theatre has a sign on it, indicating the endless possibilities of the experience. A sign called 'Jolly Hunting. Great Automobile Hunt' initiates a fantastic orgy of mechanical destruction in which Harry becomes a lustful murderer. A second sign reads: 'Guidance in the Building Up of the Personality. Success Guaranteed', which indicates a kind of chess game in which the pieces are the part of the personality. Cosmic psychotherapy. 'We demonstrate to anyone whose soul has fallen to pieces that he can rearrange these pieces of a previous self in what order he pleases, and so attain to an endless multiplicity of moves in the game of life.' Another sign reads: 'All Girls Are Yours', and carries Harry into inexhaustible sexual fantasies. The crisis of the Steppenwolf, his inner conflicts, his despair, his morbidity and unsatisfied longing are dissolved in a whirling kaleidoscope of hallucinations. 'I knew that all the hundred thousand pieces of life's game were in my pocket. A glimpse of its meaning had stirred my reason and I was determined to begin the game afresh. I would sample its tortures once more and shudder again at its senselessness. I would traverse not once more, but often, the hell of my inner being. One day I would be a better hand at the game. One day I would learn how to laugh. Pablo was waiting for me, and Mozart too.'

So Harry Haller, the Steppenwolf, had his psychedelic session, discovered instead of one reality, infinite realities within the brain. He is admitted into the select group of those who have passed through the verbal curtain into other modes of consciousness. He has joined the elite brotherhood of the illuminati.

And then what? Where do you go from there? How can the holy sense of unity and revelation be maintained? Does one sink back into the somnambulant world of rote passion, automated action, egocentricity? The poignant cry of ex-league member H.H.: 'That almost all of us – and also I, even I – should again lose myself in the soundless deserts of mapped out reality, just like officials and shop assistants who, after a party or a Sunday outing, adapt themselves again to everyday business life!' These are issues faced by everyone who has passed into a deep, trans-ego experience. How can we preserve the freshness, illuminate each second of subsequent life? How can we maintain the ecstatic oneness with others?

Throughout the ages mystical groups have formed to provide social structure and support for transcendence. The magic circle. Often secret, always persecuted by the sleepwalking majority, these cults move quietly in the background of history. The problem is, of course, the amount of structure surrounding the mystical spark. Too much too soon, and you have priesthood ritual on your hands. And the flame is gone. Too little, and the teaching function is lost; the interpersonal unity drifts into gaseous anarchy. The bohemians. The beats. The lonely arrogants.

Free from attachment to self, to social games, to anthropomorphic humanism, even to life itself, the illuminated soul can sustain the heightened charge of energy released by transcendent experiences. But such men are rare in any century. The rest of us seem to need support on the way. Men who attempt to pursue the psychedelic-drug path on their own are underestimating the power and the scope of the nervous system. A variety of LSD casualties results: breakdown, confusion, grandiosity, prima-donna individualism, disorganized eccentricity, sincere knavery, and retreat to conformity. It makes no more sense to blame the drug for such *casualties than it does to blame the nuclear process for the bomb. Would it not be more accurate to lament our primitive tribal pressures towards personal power, success, individualism?*

Huston Smith has remarked that of the eightfold path of the Buddha, the ninth and greatest is right association. The transpersonal group. The consciousness-expansion community. Surround yourself after the vision, after the psychedelic session, with friends who share the goal, who can up-level you by example or unitive love, who can help reinstate the illumination.

The sociology of transcendence. Hesse takes up the problem of the transpersonal community in the form of the League of Eastern Wayfarers.[3]

'It was my destiny to join in a great experience. Having had the good fortune to belong to the League, I was permitted to be a participant in a unique journey.' The narrator, H.H., tells that the starting place of the journey was Germany, and the time shortly after the First World War. 'Our people at that time were lured by many phantoms, but there were also many real spiritual advances. There were bacchanalian dance societies and Anabaptist groups, there was one thing after another that seemed to point to what was wonderful and beyond the veil.' There were also scientific and artistic groups engaged in the exploration of consciousness-expanding drugs. Kurt Beringer's monograph *Der Meskalinrausch*[4] describes some of the scientific experiments and the creative applications. René Daumal's novel *Le Mont Analogue*[5] is a symbolic account of a similar league journey in France. The participants were experi-

menting widely with drugs such as hashish, mescaline,
and carbon tetrachloride.

Hesse never explicitly names any drugs in his writings,
but the passages quoted earlier from the *Steppenwolf* are
fairly unequivocal in stating that some chemical was
involved and that it had a rather direct relationship to the
subsequent experience. Now, after this first enlightenment,
in *Journey to the East*, H.H. tells of subsequent visits to the
Magical Theatre.

> We not only wandered through Space, but also
> through Time. We moved towards the East, but we
> also travelled into the Middle Ages and the Golden
> Age; we roamed through Italy or Switzerland, but at
> times we also spent the night in the 10th century
> and dwelt with the patriarchs or the fairies. During
> the times I remained alone, I often found again places
> and people of my own past. I wandered with my
> former betrothed along the edges of the forest of the
> Upper Rhine, caroused with friends of my youth in
> Tübingen, in Basle or in Florence, or I was a boy
> and went with my school-friends to catch butterflies
> or to watch an otter, or my company consisted of the
> beloved characters of my books; . . . For our goal
> was not only the East, or rather the East was not
> only a country and something geographical, but it
> was the home and youth of the soul, it was everywhere
> and nowhere, it was the union of all times.

Later the link between the Steppenwolf's drug liberation
and the league becomes more specific:

When something precious and irretrievable is lost, we have the feeling of having awakened from a dream. In my case this feeling is strangely correct, for my happiness did indeed arise from the same secret as the happiness in dreams; it arose from the freedom to experience everything imaginable simultaneously, to exchange outward and inward easily, to move Time and Space about like scenes in a theatre.

Hesse is always the esoteric hand, but there seems to be little doubt that beneath the surface of his Eastern allegory runs the history of a real-life psychedelic brotherhood. The visionary experiences described in *Journey to the East* are identified by location and name of participants. A recently published biography[6] traces the connexions between these names and locations and Hesse's friends and activities at the time.

And again and again, in Swabia, at Bodensee, in Switzerland, everywhere, we met people who understood us, or were in some way thankful that we and our League and our Journey to the East existed. Amid the tramways and banks of Zürich we came across Noah's Ark guarded by several old dogs which all had the same name, and which were bravely guided across the dangerous depths of a calm period by Hans C., Noah's descendant, friend of the arts.

Hans C. Bodmer is Hesse's friend, to whom the book is dedicated, and who later bought the house in Montagnola for Hesse. He lived at the time in a house in Zurich named the Ark.

> One of the most beautiful experiences was the League's celebration in Bremgarten; the magic circle surrounded us closely there. Received by Max and Tilli, the lords of the castle. . . .

Castle Bremgarten, near Berne, was the house of Max Wassmer, where Hesse was often a guest. The 'Black King' in Winterthur refers to another friend, Georg Reinhart, to whose house, 'filled with secrets', Hesse was often invited. The names of artists and writers which occur in *Journey to the East* are all either directly the names of actual historical persons or immediately derived from them: Lauscher, Klingsor, Paul Klee, Ninon (Hesse's wife), Hugo Wolf, Brentano, Lindhorst, etc. In other words, it appears likely that the scenes described are based on the actual experiences of a very close group of friends who met in each other's homes in southern Germany and Switzerland and pursued the journey to what was 'not only a country and something geographical, but it was the home and youth of the soul, it was everywhere and nowhere, it was the union of all times'.

So the clues suggest that for a moment in 'historical reality' a writer named Hermann Hesse and his friends wandered together through the limitless pageants of expanded consciousness, down through the evolutionary archives. Then apparently H.H. loses contact, slips back to his mind and his egocentric perspectives. 'The pilgrimage had shattered . . . the magic had then vanished more and more.' He has stumbled out of the life stream into robot rationality. H.H. wants to become an author, spin in words the story of his life. 'I, in my simplicity, wanted to write the story of the league, I, who could not decipher or understand one-thousandth part of those millions of scripts, books, pictures, and references in the archives!' Archives? The cortical library?

What then was, is, the league? Is it the exoteric society with a golden-clad president, Leo, maker of ointments and herbal cures, and a speaker, and a high throne, and an extended council hall? These are but the exoteric trappings. Is not the league rather the 'procession of believers and disciples . . . incessantly . . . moving towards the East, towards the Home of Light'? The eternal stream of life ever unfolding. The unity of the evolutionary process, too easily fragmented and frozen by illusions of individuality. 'A very slow, smooth but continuous flowing or melting; . . . It seemed that, in time, all the substance from one image would flow into the other and only one would remain . . .'

Many who have made direct contact with the life process through a psychedelic or spontaneous mystical experience find themselves yearning for a social structure. Some external form to do justice to transcendental experiences. Hermann Hesse again provides us with the esoteric instructions. Look within. The league is within. So is the 2-billion-year-old historical archive, your brain. Play it out with those who will dance with you, but remember, the external differentiating forms are illusory. The union is internal. The league is in and around you at all times.

But to be human is to be rational. *Homo sapiens* wants to know. Here is the ancient tension. To be. To know. Well, the magician has a spell to weave here, too. The intellect divorced from old-fashioned neurosis, freed from ego-centricity, from semantic reification. The mind illuminated by meditation ready to play with the lawful rhythm of concepts. The bead game.

The Bead Game (Magister Ludi),[7] begun in 1931, finished eleven years later, was published six months after its completion, but in Switzerland, not Germany. 'In opposition to the present world I had to show the realm of mind and of spirit, show it as real and unconquerable; thus my work became a Utopia, the image was projected into the future, and to my surprise the world of Castalia emerged almost by itself. Without my knowledge, it was already preformed in my soul.' Thus wrote Hesse in 1955. *The Bead Game* is the synthesis and end point of Hesse's developing thought; all the strands begun in *Siddhartha, Journey to the East, Steppenwolf* are woven together into a vision of a future society of mystic game players. The 'players with pearls of glass' are an elite of intellectual mystics who, analogously to the monastic orders of the Middle Ages, have created a mountain retreat to preserve cultural and spiritual values. The core of their practice is the bead game, 'a device that comprises the complete contents and values of our culture'. The game consists in the manipulation of a complex archive of symbols and formulas, based in their structure on music and mathematics, by means of which all knowledge, science, art, and culture can be represented.

This Game of games . . . has developed into a kind of universal speech, through the medium of which the

players are enabled to express values in lucid symbols
and to place them in relation to each other. . . . A
Game can originate, for example, from a given
astronomical configuration, a theme from a Bach
fugue, a phrase of Leibnitz or from the Upanishads,
and the fundamental idea awakened can, according to
the intention and talent of the player, either proceed
further and be built up or enriched through assonances
to relative concepts. While a moderate beginner can,
through these symbols, formulate parallels between a
piece of classical music and the formula of a natural
law, the adept and Master of the Game can lead the
opening theme into the freedom of boundless com-
binations.

The old dream of a *universitas*, a synthesis of human knowledge, combining analysis and intuition, science and art,
the play of the free intellect, governed by aesthetic and
structural analogies, not by the demands of application and
technology. Again, on the intellectual plane, the problem
is always just how much structure the mind game should
have. If there are no overall goals or rules, we have ever-
increasing specialization and dispersion, breakdown in
communication, a Babel of cultures, multiple constrictions
of the range in favour of deepening the specialized field.
Psychology. If there is too much structure or over-
investment in the game goals, we have dogmatism, stifling
conformity, ever-increasing triviality of concerns, adulation
of sheer techniques, virtuosity at the expense of understanding. Psycho-analysis.

In the history of the bead game, the author explains, the practice of meditation was introduced by the League of Eastern Wayfarers in reaction against mere intellectual virtuosity. After each move in the game a period of silent meditation was observed; the origins and meanings of the symbols involved were slowly absorbed by the players. Joseph Knecht, the Game Master, whose life is described in the book, sums up the effect as follows:

> The Game, as I interpret it, encompasses the player at the conclusion of his meditation in the same way as the surface of a sphere encloses its centre, and leaves him with the feeling of having resolved the fortuitous and chaotic world into one that is symmetrical and harmonious.

Groups which attempt to apply psychedelic experiences to social living will find in the story of Castalia all the features and problems which such attempts inevitably encounter: the need for a new language or set of symbols to do justice to the incredible complexity and power of the human cerebral machinery; the central importance of maintaining direct contact with the regenerative forces of the life process through meditation or other methods of altering consciousness; the crucial and essentially insoluble problem of the relation of the mystic community to the world at large. Can the order remain an educative, spiritual force in the society, or must it degenerate through isolation and inattention to a detached, alienated group of idealists? Every major and minor social renaissance has had to face this problem. Hesse's answer is clear: the last part of the book consists of three tales, allegedly written by Knecht, describing his life in different incarnations. In each one the hero devotes himself wholeheartedly to the service and pursuit of an idealist, spiritual goal, only to recognize at the end that he has become the slave of his own delusions. In 'The Indian Life' this is clearest: Dasa, the young Brahmin, meets a yogi who asks him to fetch water; by the stream Dasa falls asleep. Later he marries, becomes a prince, has children, wages war, pursues learning, is defeated, hurt, humiliated, imprisoned, dies – and wakes up by the stream in the forest to discover that everything had been an illusion.

> Everything had been displaced in time and everything had been telescoped within the twinkling of an eye: everything was a dream, even that which had seemed dire truth and perhaps also all that which had happened previously – the story of the prince's son Dasa, his cowherd's life, his marriage, his revenge upon Nala and his sojourn with the Yogi. They were all pictures such as one may admire on a carved palace wall, where flowers, stars, birds, apes and gods can be seen portrayed in bas-relief. Was not all that which he had most recently experienced and now had before his eyes – this awakening out of his dream of prince-hood, war and prison, this standing by the spring, this water bowl which he had just shaken, along with the thoughts he was now thinking – ultimately woven of the same stuff? Was it not dream, illusion, Maya?

And what he was about to live in the future, see with his eyes and feel with his hands until death should come – was that of other stuff, of some other fashion? It was a game and a delusion, foam and dream, it was Maya, the whole beautiful, dreadful, enchanting and desperate kaleidoscope of life with its burning joys and sorrows.

The life of Joseph Knecht is described as a series of awakenings from the time he is 'called' to enter the Castalian hierarchy ('Knecht' in German means 'servant'), through his period as Magister Ludi, to his eventual renunciation of the order and the game. Castalia is essentially the league, frozen into a social institution. Again the trickster involves us in his magnificent utopian vision, the 'Game of games', only to show at the end the transience of this form as of all others. Having reached the highest position possible in the order, Knecht resigns his post. He warns the order of its lack of contact with the outside world and points out that Castalia, like any other social form, is limited in time. In his justificatory speech he refers to 'a kind of spiritual experience which I have undergone from time to time and which I call "awakening".'

I have never thought of these awakenings as manifestations of a God or a demon or even of an absolute truth. What gives them weight and credibility is not their contact with truth, their high origin, their divinity or anything in that nature, but their reality. They are monstrously real in their presence and

inescapability, like some violent bodily pain or sur-
prising natural phenomenon. . . . My life, as I saw it,
was to be a transcendence, a progress from step to
step, a series of realms to be traversed and left behind
one after another, just as a piece of music perfects,
completes and leaves behind theme after theme, tempo
after tempo, never tired, never sleeping, always
aware and always perfect in the present. I had noticed
that, coincidental with the experience of awakening,
there actually were such steps and realms, and that
each time a life stage was coming to an end it was
fraught with decay and a desire for death before
leading to a new realm, and awakening and to a new
beginning.

The mystic or visionary is always in opposition to or outside of social institutions, and even if the institution is the
most perfect imaginable, the game of games, even if it is
the one created by oneself, this too is transient, limited,
another realm to be traversed. After leaving Castalia,
Knecht wanders off on foot:

It was all perfectly new again, mysterious and of great
promise; everything that had once been could be
revived, and much that was new besides. It seemed
ages since the day and the world had looked so
beautiful, innocent and undismayed. The joy of
freedom and independence flowed through his veins
like a strong potion, and he recalled how long it was
since he had felt this precious sensation, this lovely
and enchanting illusion!

So there it is. The saga of H.H. The critics tell us that Hesse is the master novelist. Well, maybe. But the novel is a social form, and the social in Hesse is exoteric. At another level Hesse is the master guide to the psychedelic experience and its application. Before your LSD session, read *Siddhartha* and *Steppenwolf*. The last part of the *Steppenwolf* is a priceless manual.

Then when you face the problem of integrating your visions with the plastic-doll routine of your life, study *Journey to the East*. Find yourself a magic circle. League members await you on all sides. With more psychedelic experience, you will grapple with the problem of language and communication, and your thoughts and your actions will be multiplied in creative complexity as you learn how to play with the interdisciplinary symbols, the multilevel metaphors. *The bead game*.

But always, Hesse reminds us, stay close to the internal core. The mystic formulas, the league, the staggeringly rich intellectual potentials are deadening traps if the internal flame is not kept burning. The flame is of course always there, within and without, surrounding us, keeping us alive. Our only task is to keep tuned in.

Did Hesse Use Mind-Changing Drugs?

Although the argument of the preceding commentary does not depend on the answer to this question, there are sufficient clues in Hesse's writings to make the matter of some historical and literary interest. In Germany, at the time Hesse was writing, considerable research on mescaline was going on. This has been reported in a monograph by Kurt Beringer, *Der Meskalinrausch*. Much of the material was also analysed in Heinrich Klüver's monograph, *Mescal*, the first book on mescaline published in English.*

In response to our inquiry, Professor Klüver, now at the University of Chicago, has written:

> To my knowledge Hermann Hesse never took mescaline (I once raised this question in Switzerland). I do not know whether he even knew of the mescaline experiments going on under the direction of Beringer in Heidelberg. You know, of course, that Hesse (and his family) was intimately acquainted with the world and ideas of India. This no doubt has coloured many scenes in his books.

REFERENCES

1. Hermann Hesse, *Siddhartha*, trans. by Hilda Rosner (New York, New Directions, 1957), pp. 20, 144, 147, 151–3.
2. ——, *Steppenwolf*, trans. by Basil Creighton (New York, Random House, 1963), pp. vi, 62, 63, 66–7, 197–9, 217, 246.
3. ——, *The Journey to the East*, trans. by Hilda Rosner (New York, Noonday Press, 1957), pp. 3, 10, 27–8, 29, 31, 96, 118.
4. Kurt Beringer, *Der Meskalinrausch, seine Geschichte und Erscheinungsweise* (Berlin, Springer, 1927).
5. René Daumal, *Mount Analogue: An Authentic Narrative*, trans. and intro. by Roger Shattuck; postface by Véra Daumal (New York, Pantheon, 1960).

Mescal: The 'Divine' Plant and Its Psychological Effects (University of Chicago Press, 1964).

6. Bernhard Zeller, *Hermann Hesse: Eine Chronik in Bildern* (Frankfurt, Suhrkamp, 1960).

7. Hermann Hesse, *Magister Ludi (The Bead Game)*, trans. by Mervyn Savill (New York, Ungar, 1957), pp. 10, 17, 39, 355–6, 359, 367, 500–501.

The Journey to the East

One

As it has been my destiny to take part in a great experience, and having had the good fortune to belong to the League and allowed to share in that unique journey, the wonder of which blazed like a meteor and afterwards sank into oblivion – even falling into disrepute – I have now decided to attempt a short description of this incredible journey. No man since the days of Hugo and mad Roland has ventured upon such a journey, until our own remarkable times; the troubled, confused, yet so fruitful period following the Great War.

I have allowed myself no illusions as to the difficulties involved in such an attempt. They are very great, and are not only subjective, although these in themselves would be considerable enough. For not only do I no longer possess the tokens, mementos, documents and diaries relating to the journey, but in the difficult years of misfortune, sickness and deep affliction which have elapsed since then, many of my recollections have also vanished. As a result of the blows of Fate and continual discouragement, my memory as well as my confidence in these earlier vivid recollections have become impaired. But apart from these purely personal notes, I am handicapped because of my former vow to the League; for although this vow permits unrestricted communication of my personal experiences, it forbids any disclosures about the League itself. And even though the League seems to have had no visible existence for a long time and I have not seen any of its members again, no allurement or threat in the world would induce me to break my vow. On the contrary, if today or tomorrow I had to appear before a court-martial and was given the option of dying or divulging the secret of the League, I would joyously seal my vow to the League with death.

It can be noted here that since the travel diary of Count Keyserling, several books have appeared in which the authors, partly unconsciously, but also partly deliberately, have given the impression that they are brothers of the League and had taken part in the Journey to the East. Incidentally, even the adventurous travel accounts of Ossendowski come under this justifiable suspicion. But they have nothing to do with the League and our Journey to the East any more than ministers of a small sanctimonious sect have to do with the Saviour, the Apostles and the Holy Ghost to whom they refer for special favour and membership. Even if Count Keyserling really sailed round the world with ease, and if Ossendowski actually traversed the countries he described, yet their journeys were not remarkable and they discovered no new territory, whereas at certain stages of our Journey to the East, although the commonplace aids of modern travel such as railways, steamers, telegraph, automobiles, aeroplanes, etc., were renounced, we penetrated into the heroic and magical.

It was shortly after the Great War, and the beliefs of the conquered nations were in an extraordinary state of unreality. There was a readiness to believe in things beyond reality even though only a few barriers were actually overcome and few advances made into the realm of a

future psychiatry. Our journey at that time across the
Moon Ocean to Famagusta under the leadership of Albert
the Great, or say, the discovery of the Butterfly Island,
twelve leagues beyond Zipangu, or the inspiring league
ceremony at Rudiger's grave – those were deeds and experiences which were allotted once only to people of our
time and zone.

I see that I am already coming up against one of the
greatest obstacles in my account. The heights to which our
deeds rose, the spiritual plane of experience to which they
belong might be made proportionately more comprehen-
sible to the reader if it were permitted to disclose to him
the essence of the League's secret. But a great deal, perhaps
everything, will remain incredible and incomprehensible to
him. The paradox alone must always be accepted that the
seemingly impossible must continually be attempted. I
agree with Siddhartha, our wise friend from the East, who
once said: 'Words do not express thoughts very well;
everything immediately becomes a little different, a little
distorted, a little foolish. And yet it also pleases me and
seems right that what is of value and wisdom to one man
seems nonsense to another.' Even centuries ago the
members and historians of our League recognised and
courageously faced up to this difficulty. One of the greatest
of them gave expression to it in an immortal verse:

'He who travels far will often see things
Far removed from what he believed was Truth.
When he talks about it in the fields at home,
He is often accused of lying,

For the obdurate people will not believe
What they do not see and distinctly feel.
Inexperience, I believe,
Will give little credence to my song.'

This 'inexperience' has given rise to the position where our journey, which once raised thousands to a state of ecstasy, has not only been forgotten by the public, but a real taboo has been placed upon its memory. History is rich in examples of a similar kind. The whole of world history often seems to me nothing more than a picture-book which portrays humanity's most powerful and senseless desire – the desire to forget. Does not each generation, by means of suppression, concealment and ridicule, efface what the previous generation considered most important? Have we not just had the experience that a long, horrible, monstrous war has been forgotten, distorted and dismissed by every nation? And now that they have had a short respite, are not the same nations trying to recall by means of exciting war novels what they themselves caused and endured a few years ago? In the same way, the day of rediscovery will come for the deeds and sorrows of our League, which are now either forgotten or are a laughing-stock in the world, and my notes should make a small contribution towards it.

One of the characteristics of the Journey to the East was that although the League aspired to quite definite, very lofty aims during this journey (they belong to the secret category and therefore cannot be revealed), nevertheless each member could have his own private aims and indeed without them he would not have been included in the party. Each of us, although he appeared to share common ideals and aims, was borne up and comforted by his own fond childhood dream deep within his heart as a source of inner strength and comfort. My own goal for the journey, about which the President questioned me before my acceptance into the League, was a simple one, but many members of the League had set themselves goals which, although I respected, I could not fully understand. For example, one of them was a treasure-seeker and he thought of nothing else but of winning a great treasure which he called 'Tao'. Still another had conceived the idea of capturing a certain snake to which he attributed magical powers and which he called Kundalini. My own journey and life-goal, which had coloured my dreams since my late boyhood, was to see the beautiful Princess Fatima and, if possible, to win her love.

When I had the good fortune to join the League – that is, immediately after the end of the Great War – our country was full of saviours, prophets and disciples; of presentiments about the end of the world, or hopes for the dawn of a Third Empire. Shattered by the war, in despair as a result of deprivation and hunger, greatly disillusioned by the seeming futility of all the sacrifices in blood and property, our people were exposed to many chimeras, but at the same time many real spiritual advances were made. There were Bacchanalian dance societies and Anabaptist groups, there was one thing after another that seemed to point to what was wonderful and beyond the veil. There was also at that time a widespread leaning

towards Indian, ancient Persian and other Eastern
mysteries and religions, and all this gave most people the
impression that our ancient League was one of the many
newly-blossomed cults, and that after a few years it also
would be half-forgotten, despised and decried. The faithful
amongst its disciples cannot dispute this.

How well I remember presenting myself, after the ex-
piration of my probation year, before the High Throne.
The aim of the Journey to the East was revealed to me and
after I had dedicated myself, body and soul, to this project,
I was asked in a friendly way what I personally hoped to
gain from this journey into the legendary realm. Colouring
slightly, I confessed frankly and unhesitatingly to the
assembled officials that it was my heart's desire to be
allowed to see Princess Fatima. The Speaker, interpreting
the allusion, gently placed his hand on my head and
uttered the formula which confirmed my admission as a
member of the League. 'Anima pia,' he said and bade me
be constant in faith, courageous in danger, and to love my
fellow-men. Well-schooled during my year's probation, I
took the oath, renounced the world and its superstitions
and had the League ring placed on my finger to the words
from one of the most beautiful chapters in our League's
history:

> 'On earth and in the air, in water and in fire,
> The spirits are subservient to him,
> His glance frightens and tames the wildest beasts,
> And even the anti-Christian must approach him
> with awe... etc.'

To my great pleasure, immediately on admission to the League, we novitiates were told about our prospects. For instance, on following the directions of the officials to join one of the groups of ten people travelling throughout the country to join the League's expedition, one of the League's secrets immediately became vividly clear to me. I realised that I had joined a pilgrimage to the East, seemingly a definite and single pilgrimage – but in reality, in its broadest sense, this expedition to the East was not only mine and now; this procession of believers and disciples had always and incessantly been moving towards the East, towards the Home of Light. Throughout the centuries it had been on the way, towards light and wonder, and each member, each group, indeed our whole host and its great pilgrimage, was only a wave in the eternal stream of human beings, of the eternal strivings of the human spirit towards the East, towards Home. The knowledge passed through my mind like a ray of light and immediately reminded me of a phrase which I had learned during my novitiate year, which had always pleased me immensely without my realising its full significance. It was a phrase by the poet Novalis, 'Where are we really going? Always home!'

Meantime, our group had set off on its travels; soon we encountered other groups, and the feeling of unity and a common goal gave us increasing happiness. Faithful to our instructions, we lived like pilgrims and made no use of those contrivances which spring into existence in a world deluded by money, time and figures, and which drain life of all meaning; mechanical contrivances such as railways,

watches and the like came chiefly into this category.
Another unanimously observed rule bade us visit and pay
homage to all places and associations relating to the ancient
history of our League and its faith. We visited and honoured
all sacred places and monuments, churches and consecrated
tombstones which we came across on our way; chapels and
altars were adorned with flowers; ruins were honoured
with songs or silent contemplation; the dead were com-
memorated with music and prayers. It was not unusual for
us to be mocked at and disturbed by unbelievers, but it also
happened often enough that priests blessed us and invited
us to be their guests, that children enthusiastically joined
us, learned our songs and saw us depart with tears in their
eyes, that an old man would show us forgotten monuments
or tell us a legend about his district; that young men would
walk with us part of the way and wish to join the League.
The latter were given advice and taught the first rites and
practices of novitiates.

We were aware of the first wonders, partly through
seeing them with our own eyes and partly through unexpected accounts and legends. One day, when I was still
quite a new member, someone suddenly mentioned that
the giant Agramant was a guest in our leaders' tent, and
was trying to persuade them to make their way across
Africa in order to liberate some League members from
Moorish captivity. Another time we saw the Goblin, the
pitchmaker, the comforter, and we presumed that we
should make our way towards the Blue Pot. However, the
first amazing phenomenon which I saw with my own eyes
was when we had stopped for prayer and rest at an old

half-ruined Chapel in the region of Spaichendorf; on the only undamaged wall of the Chapel there was painted a very large picture of Saint Christopher, and on his shoulder, small, and half-faded from old age, sat the Child Saviour. The leaders, as was sometimes their custom, did not simply propose the direction we should take, but invited us all to give our opinion, for the Chapel lay at a three-direction signpost and we had the choice. Only a few of us expressed a wish or gave advice, but one person pointed to the left and urgently requested that we should choose this path. We all remained silent and were awaiting our leaders' decision, when Saint Christopher raised his arm holding the long, thick staff and pointed to the left where our brother desired to go. We watched in silence, and silently the leaders turned to the left and went along this path, and we all followed with the utmost pleasure.

We had not been long on our way in Swabia when a power which we had not thought about became noticeable. We had felt its influence strongly for some time without quite knowing whether it was friendly or hostile. It was the power of the guardians of the crown who, since olden times, had preserved the memory and inheritance of the Hohenstaufen in that country. I do not know whether our leaders knew more about it and had any instructions regarding it. I only know that we received many exhortations and warnings from them, such as on the hill on the way to Bopfingen where we met a hoary old warrior; he shook his grey head with his eyes closed and disappeared again without trace. Our leaders took notice of the warning; we turned back and did not go to Bopfingen. On the other hand, it happened in the neighbourhood of Urach that an ambassador of the crown guardians appeared in our leaders' tent as if sprung from out of the ground, and with promises and threats tried to induce them to put our expedition at the service of the Staufen, and indeed to make preparations for the conquest of Sicily. When the leaders firmly refused this demand, he said he would put a dreadful curse on the League and on our expedition. And yet I am only reporting what was whispered among ourselves; the leaders themselves did not mention a word about it. Still, it seems possible that it was our uncertain relationship with the guardians of the crown which, for a long time, gave our League the unmerited reputation of being a secret society for the restoration of the monarchy.

On one occasion I also had the experience of seeing one of my comrades entertain doubts; he renounced his vow and relapsed into disbelief. He was a young man whom I had liked very much. His personal reason for joining the expedition to the East was his desire to see the coffin of the prophet Mohammed from which, it had been said, he could by magic rise freely into the air. In one of those Swabian or Alemannic small towns where we stopped for a few days, because an opposition of Saturn and the moon checked our progress, this unfortunate man, who had seemed sad and restless for some time, met one of his former teachers to whom he had remained very attached since his schooldays. This teacher was successful in again making the young man see our cause in the light which it appears to unbelievers. After one of these visits to the teacher, the poor man came back to our camp in a dreadful state of excitement, his face distorted. He made a commotion outside the leaders' tent, and when the Speaker came out he shouted at him angrily that he had had enough of this ridiculous expedition which would never bring us to the East; he had had enough of the journey being interrupted for days because of stupid astrological considerations; he was more than tired of idleness, of childish wanderings, of floral ceremonies, of attaching importance to magic, of the intermingling of life and poetry; he would throw the ring at the leaders' feet, take his leave and return by the trusty railway to his home and his useful work. It was an ugly and lamentable sight. We were filled with shame and yet at the same time pitied the misguided man. The Speaker listened to him kindly, stooped with a smile for the discarded ring, and said in a quiet, cheerful voice which must have put the blustering man to shame: 'You have said good-bye to us and want to return to the railway, to common-sense and useful work. You have said good-bye to the League, to the expedition to the East, good-bye to magic, to floral festivals, to poetry. You are absolved from your vow.'

'Also from the vow of silence?' cried the deserter.

'Yes, also from the vow of silence,' answered the Speaker. 'Remember, you vowed to keep silent about the secret of the League to unbelievers. As we see you have forgotten the secret, you will not be able to pass it on to anyone.'

'I have forgotten something? I have forgotten nothing!' cried the young man, but became uncertain, and as the

Speaker turned his back on him and withdrew to the tent, he suddenly ran quickly away.

We were sorry, but the days were crammed so full with events that I quickly forgot him. But it happened some time later, when none of us thought about him any more, that we heard the inhabitants of several villages and towns through which we passed, talk about this same youth. A young man had been there (and they described him accurately and mentioned his name) who had been looking for us everywhere. First he had said that he belonged to us, had stayed behind on the journey and had lost his way. Then he began to weep and stated that he had been unfaithful to us and had run away, but now he realised that he could no longer live outside the League; he wished to, and indeed must, find us in order to go down on his knees before the leaders and beg to be forgiven. We heard this tale told again here, there, and everywhere; wherever we went, the wretched man had just been there. We asked the Speaker what he thought about it and what would be the outcome. 'I do not think that he will find us,' said the Speaker briefly. And he did not find us. We did not see him again.

Once, when one of the leaders had drawn me into a confidential conversation, I gathered courage and asked him how things stood with this renegade brother. After all, he was penitent and was looking for us, I said; we ought to help him redeem his error. No doubt he would in the future be the most loyal member of the League. The leader said: 'We should be happy if he did find his way back to us, but we cannot help him. He has made it very difficult for himself to have faith again. I fear that he would not see and recognise us even if we passed close by him; he has become blind. Repentance alone does not help. Grace cannot be bought with repentance; it cannot be bought at all. A similar thing has already happened to many other people; great and famous men have shared the same fate as this young man. Once in their youth the light shone for them; they saw the light and followed the star, but then came reason and the mockery of the world; then came faint-heartedness and apparent failure; then came weariness and disillusion, and so they lost their way again, they became blind once more. Some of them have spent the rest of their lives looking for us again, but could not find us. They have then told the world that our League is only a pretty legend and people should not be misled by it. Others have become our deadly enemies and have abused and harmed the League in every possible way.'

There were wonderful festive days whenever we met other parties of the League's hosts on our way; sometimes we then formed a camp of hundreds, even thousands. The expedition did not, in fact, proceed in any fixed order with everyone moving in the same direction in more or less closed columns. On the contrary, numerous groups were simultaneously on the move, each following their own leaders and their own stars, each one always ready to merge into a greater unit and belong to it for a time, but equally prepared to move on again separately. Some went on their way quite alone. I also walked alone at times, whenever some sign or call tempted me to go my own way.

I remember a select little group with which we travelled

and camped for some days; this group had undertaken to liberate some captive League brothers and the Princess Isabella from the hands of the Moors. It was said that they were in possession of Hugo's horn, and among them were my friends the poet Lauscher and the artists Klingsor and Paul Klee; they spoke of nothing else but Africa and the captured princess, and their Bible was the book of the deeds of Don Quixote, in whose honour they thought of making their way across Spain.

It was very pleasant whenever we met one of these groups, to attend their feasts and devotions and to invite them to ours, to hear about their deeds and plans, to bless and know them on parting; they went their way, we went ours. Each one of them had his own dream, his wish, his secret heart's desire, and yet they all flowed together in the great stream and all belonged to each other, shared the same reverence and the same faith, and had made the same vow! I met Jup, the magician, who hoped to find the greatest happiness of his life in Kashmir; I met Collofine, the sorcerer, quoting his favourite passage from the Adventures of Simplicissimus; I met Louis the Terrible, who dreamt of planting an olive-grove in the Holy Land and keeping slaves. He went arm-in-arm with Anselm, who was in search of the purple iris of his childhood. I met and loved Ninon, known as 'the foreigner'. Dark eyes gleamed beneath her black hair. She was jealous of Fatima, the princess of my dreams, and yet she was probably Fatima herself without my knowing it. And as we moved on, so had once pilgrims, emperors and crusaders moved on to liberate the Saviour's grave, or to study

Arabian magic; Spanish knights had travelled this way, as well as German scholars, Irish monks and French poets.

I, whose calling was really only that of a violinist and story-teller, was responsible for the provision of music for our group, and I then discovered how a long time devoted to small details exalts us and increases our strength. I did not only play the violin and conduct our choirs, but also collected old songs and chorals. I wrote motets and madrigals for six and eight voices and practised them. But I will not give you details of these.

I was very fond of many of my comrades and leaders, but not one of them subsequently occupied my thoughts as much as Leo, while at that time he was apparently hardly noticed. Leo was one of our servants (who were naturally volunteers, as we were). He helped to carry the luggage and was often assigned to the personal service of the Speaker. This unaffected man had something so pleasing, so unobtrusively winning about him that everyone loved him. He did his work gaily, usually sang or whistled as he went along, was never seen except when needed – in fact, an ideal servant. Furthermore, all animals were attached to him. We nearly always had some dog or other with us which joined us on account of Leo; he could tame birds and attract butterflies to him. His desire was for Solomon's key which would enable him to understand the language of the birds that had drawn him to the East. By comparison with some of the many forms of our League, which without detracting from its value and sincerity, were nevertheless rather exaggerated, bizarre, solemn or fantastic, Leo the servant seemed so simple and natural, so glowing with health, and so unassumingly friendly.

What makes my account particularly difficult is the great disparity in my individual recollections. I have already said that sometimes we marched along only as a small group; sometimes we formed a troop or even an army, but sometimes I remained in a district with only a few friends, or even quite alone, without tents, without leaders and without a Speaker. My tale becomes even more difficult because we not only wandered through Space, but also through Time. We moved towards the East, but we also travelled into the Middle ages and the Golden Age; we roamed through Italy or Switzerland, but at times we also spent the night in the tenth century and dwelt with the patriarchs or the fairies. During the times I remained alone, I often found again places and people of my own past. I wandered with my former betrothed along the edges of the forest of the Upper Rhine, caroused with friends of my youth in Tübingen, in Basle or in Florence, or I was a boy and went with my school-friends to catch butterflies or to watch an otter, or my company consisted of the beloved characters of my books; Almansor and Parsifal, Witiko or Goldmund rode by my side, or Sancho Panza, or we were guests at the Barmekides. When I found my way back to our group in some valley or other, heard the League's songs and camped by the leaders' tents, it was immediately clear to me that my excursion into my childhood and my ride with Sancho belonged essentially to this journey. For our goal was not only the East, or rather the East was not only a country and something geographical,

but it was the home and youth of the soul, it was everywhere and nowhere, it was the union of all times. Yet I
was only aware of this for a moment, and therein lay the
reason for my great happiness at that time. Later, when I
had lost this happiness, I clearly understood these connec-
tions without deriving the slightest benefit or comfort
from them. When something precious and irretrievable is
lost, we feel we have awakened from a dream. In my case
this feeling is strangely correct, for my happiness did
indeed arise from the same secret as the happiness in
dreams; it arose from the freedom to experience everything
imaginable simultaneously, to exchange outward and
inward easily, to move Time and Space about like scenes in
a theatre. And as we League brothers travelled throughout
the world without motor-cars or ships, as we conquered the
war-shattered world by our faith and transformed it into
Paradise, we creatively brought the past, the future and the
fictitious into the present moment.

Again and again, in Swabia, at Bodensee, in Switzerland,
everywhere, we met people who understood us, or were in
some way thankful that we and our League and our Journey
to the East existed. Amid the tramways and banks of
Zürich we came across Noah's Ark guarded by several old
dogs which all had the same name, and which were bravely
guided across the shallow waters of a calm period by Hans
C. to Noah's descendant, to the friend of the arts. We
went to Winterthur, down into Stocklin's Magic Closet;
we were guests in the Chinese Temple where the incense
holders gleamed beneath the bronze Maja and the black
king played the flute sweetly to the vibrating tone of the

temple gong. And at the foot of the Sun Mountains we came across Suon Mali, a colony of the King of Siam, where, amongst the stone and brazen Buddhas, we offered up our libations and incense as grateful guests.

One of the most beautiful experiences was the League's celebration in Bremgarten; the magic circle surrounded us closely there. Received by Max and Tilli, the lords of the castle, we heard Othmar play Mozart on the grand piano in the lofty hall. We found the grounds occupied by parrots and other talking birds. We heard the fairy Armida sing at the fountain. With blown locks the heavy head of the astrologer Longus nodded by the side of the beloved countenance of Henry of Ofterdingen. In the garden, the peacocks screeched, and Louis conversed in Spanish with Puss in Boots, while Hans Resom, shaken after his peeps into the masked game of life, vowed he would go on a pilgrimage to the grave of Charles the Great. It was one of the triumphant periods of our journey; we had brought the magic wave with us; it cleansed everything. The inhabitants knelt and worshipped beauty, the lord of the castle recited a poem telling of our deeds on the previous day. The animals from the forest lurked close to the castle walls, and in the river the gleaming fishes moved in lively swarms and were fed with cakes and wine.

The best of these experiences really worth relating are those which reflect the spirit of it. My description of them seems poor and perhaps foolish, but everyone who shared in and celebrated the days at Bremgarten would confirm every single detail and supplement them with hundreds which are more beautiful. I shall always remember how the peacocks' tails shimmered when the moon rose amongst the tall trees, and on the shady bank the emerging mermaids gleamed fresh and silvery amongst the rocks; how Don Quixote stood alone under the chestnut-tree by the fountain and held his first nightwatch while the last Roman candles of the firework display fell so softly over the castle's turrets in the moonlight, and my colleague Pablo, adorned with roses, played the Persian reed-pipe to the girls. Oh, which of us ever thought that the magic circle would break up so soon! That almost all of us – and also I, even I – should again be lost in the soundless deserts of mapped-out reality, just like officials and shop-assistants who, after a party or a Sunday outing, adapt themselves again to everyday business life!

In those days none of us was capable of such thoughts. From the castle's turrets of Bremgarten, the fragrance of lilac entered my bedroom. I heard the river flowing beyond the trees. I climbed out of the window in the depth of the night, intoxicated with happiness and yearning. I stole past the knight on guard and the sleeping banqueters down to the river-bank, to the flowing waters, to the white, gleaming mermaids. They took me down with them into the cool, moonlit crystal world of their home, where they played dreamily with the crowns and golden chains from their treasure-chambers. It seemed to me that I spent months in the sparkling depths, yet when I emerged and swam ashore, thoroughly refreshed, Pablo's reed-pipe was still to be heard from the garden far away, and the moon was still high in the sky. I saw Leo playing with two white poodles, his clever, boyish face radiating happiness. I found Longus sitting in the wood. On his knees was a book of parchment in which he was writing Greek and Hebrew characters; dragons flew out of the letters, and coloured snakes reared up. He did not look at me; he went on painting, absorbed in his coloured snake-writing. For a long time I looked over his bent shoulders into the book. I saw the snakes and dragons emerge from his writing whirl about and silently disappear into the dark wood. 'Longus,' I said to him softly, 'dear friend!' He did not hear me, my world was far from his. And quite apart, under the moonlit trees, Anselm wandered about with an iris in his hand; lost in thought, he stared and smiled at the flower's purple calyx.

Something that I had observed several times during our journey, without having fully considered it, impressed me again during the days at Bremgarten, strangely and rather painfully. There were amongst us many artists, painters, musicians and poets. Ardent Klingsor was there and restless Hugo Wolf, taciturn Lauscher and vivacious Brentano – but however animated and lovable the personalities of these artists were, yet without exception their imaginary characters were more animated, more beautiful, happier and certainly finer and more real than the poets and creators themselves. Pablo sat there with his flute in enchanting innocence and joy, but his poet slipped away like a shadow to the river-bank, half-transparent in the moonlight, seeking solitude. Stumbling and rather drunk, Hoffman ran here and there amongst the guests, talking a great deal, small and elfish, and he also, like all of them, was only half-real, only half there, not quite solid, not quite real. At the same time, the archivist Lindhorst, playing at dragons for a joke, continually breathed fire and discharged energy like an automobile. I asked the servant Leo why it was that artists sometimes appeared to be only half-alive, while their creations seemed so irrefutably alive. Leo looked at me, surprised at my question. Then he released the poodle he was holding in his arms and said: 'It is just the same with mothers. When they have borne their children and given them their milk and beauty and strength, they themselves become insignificant and no one asks about them any more.'

'But that is sad,' I said, without really thinking very much about it.

'I do not think it is more sad than all other things,' said Leo. 'Perhaps it is sad and yet also beautiful. The law ordains that it shall be so.'

'The law?' I asked curiously. 'Which law is that, Leo?'

'It is the law of service. He who wishes to live long must serve, but he who wishes to rule does not live long.'

'Then why do so many strive to rule?'

'Because they do not understand. There are few who are born to be masters; they remain happy and healthy. But all the others who have only become masters through endeavour, end in nothing.'

'In what nothing, Leo?'

'In a sanatorium, for example.'

I understood little about it and yet the words remained in my memory and left me with a feeling that this Leo knew all kinds of things, that he perhaps knew more than us, who were ostensibly his masters.

Two

Each traveller on this unforgettable journey had his own ideas as to what made our faithful Leo suddenly decide to leave us in the middle of the dangerous gorge of Morbio Inferiore. It was only very much later that I began in some measure to suspect and review the circumstances and deeper significance of this occurrence. It also seemed that this apparently incidental but in reality extremely important event, the disappearance of Leo, was in no way an accident, but a link in that chain of events through which the eternal enemy sought to bring disaster to our undertaking. On that cool autumn morning when it was discovered that our servant Leo was missing and that all search for him remained fruitless, I was certainly not the only one who, for the first time, had a feeling of impending disaster and menacing destiny.

However, for the moment, this was the position. After we had boldly crossed half Europe and a portion of the Middle Ages, we camped in a very narrow rocky valley, a wild mountain gorge on the Italian border, and looked for the inexplicably missing Leo. The longer we looked for him and the more our hopes of finding him again dwindled as the day went on, the more oppressed we became by the thought that it was not only the question of a popular, pleasant man amongst our servants who had either met with an accident or run away or had been captured by an enemy – but that this was the beginning of trouble, the first indication of a storm which would break over us.

We spent all day, far into the twilight, searching for Leo. The whole of the gorge was explored, and while these exertions made us weary, and a feeling of hopelessness and futility grew amongst us all, it was both strange and uncanny how from hour to hour the missing servant seemed to increase in importance and our loss created difficulties. It was not only that each pilgrim, and certainly all the staff, were worried about the handsome, pleasant and willing youth, but it seemed that the more certain his loss became, the more indispensable he seemed; without Leo, his handsome face, his good humour and his songs, without his enthusiasm for our great undertaking, the undertaking itself seemed in some mysterious way to lose meaning. At least, that is how it affected me. Despite all the strain and many minor disillusionments during the previous months of the journey, I had never had a moment of inner weakness, of serious doubt; no successful general, no bird in the swallows' flight to Egypt, could be more sure of his goal, of his mission, of the rightness of his actions and aspirations than I was on this journey. But now, in this fateful place, while I continually heard the calls and signals of our sentinels during the whole of the blue and golden October day, and awaited again and again with growing excitement the arrival of news, only to suffer disappointment and to look round at perplexed faces, I had feelings of sadness and doubt for the first time. The stronger these feelings became, the clearer it seemed to me that it was not only that I had lost faith in finding Leo again, but everything now seemed to become unreliable and doubtful; the value and meaning of everything was threatened: our comradeship, our faith, our vow, our Journey to the East, our whole life.

Even if I was mistaken in presuming that we all had these feelings, indeed even if I was subsequently mistaken about my own feelings and inner experiences and many things which were in reality experienced much later and erroneously attributed to that day, there still remains, despite everything, the strange fact about Leo's luggage. Quite apart from all personal moods, this was, in fact, rather strange, fantastic, and an increasing source of worry. Even during this day in the Morbio gorge, even during our eager search for the missing man, first one man, then another missed something important, something in-dispensable from the luggage which could not be found anywhere. It appeared that every missing article must have been in Leo's luggage, and although Leo, like all the rest of us, had only carried the usual linen haversack on his back, just one bag amongst about thirty others, it seemed that in this one lost bag there were all the really important things which we carried with us on our journey.

It is a well-known human weakness that anything we lose assumes an exaggerated value and seems less dispens-able than those things still in our possession. Yet although many of the articles, whose loss in the Morbio gorge troubled us so much, did in fact turn up later or prove themselves to be unimportant; nevertheless it is un-fortunately true that we were at the time justifiably alarmed at the loss of many extremely important things.

The further extraordinary and singular thing was this: the objects that were missing, whether they appeared again later or not, assumed their importance by degrees, and gradually all the things believed lost, which we had wrongly missed so much and to which we had mistakenly attached so much importance, turned up again in our stores. In order to express here quite clearly what was true yet altogether inexplicable, it must be said that during the course of our further journey, tools, valuables, cards and documents which were all lost seemed, to our shame, to be indispensable. Quite frankly, it seemed as if each one of us stretched his entire imagination to persuade himself of terrible, irreplaceable losses, as if each one endeavoured to conceive as lost whatever was most important to him and to mourn over it; with one it was the passports, with another the maps, with another it was the Letter of Credit to the Caliph; it was this thing with one, that thing with another. And although in the end it was clear that one article after the other which was believed lost was either not lost at all or was unimportant or dispensable, there did remain one single thing that was really valuable, an inestimably important, absolutely fundamental and indispensable document that was really indisputably lost.

Opinions were now ineffectually exchanged as to whether this document, which had disappeared with the servant Leo, had really been in our luggage. There was complete agreement about the great value of this document and that it was irreplaceable, and yet how few of us (amongst them myself) could declare with certainty that this document had been taken with us on the journey. One man asserted that a similar document had certainly been carried in Leo's linen bag; this was not the original document at all, but naturally only a copy; others declared that it had never been intended to take either the document itself or a copy on the journey, as this would have made a mockery of the whole meaning of our journey. This led to heated arguments and further demonstrated that there were various completely conflicting opinions about the whereabouts of the original (it was immaterial whether we only had the copy and whether we had lost it or not). The document, it was declared, was deposited with the government in Kyffhäuser. No, said another, it lies buried in the urn which contains the ashes of our deceased master. Nonsense, said still another, the League document was drawn up by the master in the original characters known only to himself and it was burned with the master's corpse at his behest. Enquiries regarding the original document were meaningless, because after the master's death it was not possible for anyone to read it. But it was certainly necessary to ascertain where the four (some said six) translations of the original document were, which were made during the master's lifetime under his supervision. It was said that Chinese, Greek, Hebrew and Latin translations existed, and they were deposited in the four old capitals. Many other opinions and views were expressed; many clung obstinately to them, others were convinced first by one then by another opposing argument, and then soon changed their minds again. In brief, from that time, certainty and unity no longer existed in our community, although the great idea still kept us together.

How well do I remember those first disputes! They were something so new and unheard-of in our hitherto perfectly united League. They were conducted with respect and politeness – at least at the beginning. At first they led neither to fierce conflicts nor personal reproaches or insults – at first we were still an inseparable, united brotherhood throughout the world. I still hear their voices, I still see our camping ground where the first of these debates was conducted. I see the golden autumn leaves falling here and there amongst the unusually serious faces. I see one on a knee, another lying on a hat. I listened, feeling more and more distressed and fearful, but amidst all the exchange of opinions I was inwardly quite sure of my belief, sadly sure; namely, that the original, genuine document had been in Leo's bag, and that it had disappeared and was lost with him. However gloomy, still it was a belief. It was a firm one and gave me a feeling of certainty. At that time I truly thought that I would willingly exchange this conviction for a more hopeful one. Only later, when I had lost this as well and was susceptible to all kinds of opinions, did I realise what I had possessed in my belief.

I see that the tale cannot be told in this way. But how can it be told, this tale of a unique journey, of a unique communion of minds, of such a wonderfully exalted and spiritual life? I should like so very much, as one of the last survivors of our community, to save some records of our great cause. I feel like the old surviving servant of perhaps one of the Paladins of Charles the Great, who recalls a stirring series of deeds and wonders, the images and memories of which will disappear with him if he is not successful in passing some of them on to posterity by means of word or picture, tale or song. But in which medium is it possible for the story of the Journey to the East to be told? I do not know. Already this first attempt, begun with the best intentions, leads me into the boundless and incomprehensible. I simply wanted to try to depict what I have remembered of the course of events and individual details of our Journey to the East. Nothing seemed more simple. And now, when I have scarcely begun, I am brought to a halt by a single small episode which I had not originally thought of at all, the episode of Leo's disappearance. Instead of a fabric, I hold in my hands a bundle of a thousand knotted threads which would occupy hundreds of hands for years to disentangle and straighten out, even if every thread did not become terribly brittle and break between the fingers as soon as it is handled and gently teased out.

I imagine that every historian is similarly affected when he begins to record the events of some period and wishes to portray them sincerely. Where is the centre of events, the common standpoint around which they revolve and which gives them cohesion? In order that something like cohesion, something like causality, that some kind of meaning might be revealed and that it can in some way be told, the historian must invent units, a hero, a nation, an idea, and he must allow to happen to this invented unit what has in reality happened to the nameless.

If it is so difficult to relate connectedly a number of events which have really taken place and have been attested, it is in my case much more difficult, for everything becomes questionable as soon as I consider it closely, everything slips away and dissolves just as our community, the strongest in the world, has been able to dissolve. There is no unit, no centre, no point around which the wheel revolves.

Our Journey to the East and our League, the basis of our community, has been the most important thing, indeed the only important thing in my life, compared with which my own individual life has appeared completely unimportant. And now that I want to hold fast to and describe this most important thing, or at least something of it, everything is only a mass of separate fragmentary pictures which has been reflected in something, and this something is myself, and this self, this mirror, whenever I have gazed into it, has proved to be nothing but the uppermost surface of a glass plane. I put my pen away with the sincere intention and hope of continuing tomorrow or some other time, or rather to make a fresh start, but at the back of my intention and hope, at the back of my really tremendous urge to tell our story, there remains a dreadful doubt. It is the doubt that arose during the search for Leo in the valley of Morbio. This doubt does not only ask the question, 'Can your story be told?' It also asks 'Was it possible to experience it?' We remember men who took part in the Great War who, although by no means short of facts and attested stories, must at times have entertained the same doubts.

Three

Since I wrote the foregoing, I have thought about my project again and again and tried to find a way out of my difficulty. I have not found a solution. I am still confronted by chaos. But I have vowed not to give in, and at the moment of making this vow a happy memory passed through my mind like a ray of sunshine. It was similar, it seemed to me, quite similar to how I felt when we began our expedition; then we also undertook something apparently impossible, then we also apparently travelled in the dark, not knowing our direction and without prospects. Yet we had within us something stronger than reality or probability, and that was faith in the meaning and necessity of our action. I shuddered at the recollection of this sentiment, and at the moment of this blissful shudder, everything became clear, everything seemed possible again.

Whatever happens, I have decided to exercise my will. Even if I have to re-commence my difficult story ten times, a hundred times, and always arrive at the same cul-de-sac, then I must begin again a hundred times. If I cannot assemble the pictures into a significant whole again, I will present each single fragment as faithfully as possible. And as far as it is now still possible, I will be mindful of the first principle of our great period, never to rely on and let myself be disconcerted by reason, always to know that faith is stronger than so-called reality.

In the meantime, I did make a sincere attempt to approach my goal in a practical and sensible manner. I went to see a friend of my youth who lives in this town and is editor of a newspaper. His name is Lukas. He had taken part in the Great War and had published a book about it which had a wide sale. Lukas received me in a friendly manner. He was obviously pleased to see a former school-friend again. I had two long conversations with him.

I tried to make him understand my position. I scorned all evasion. I told him frankly that I had taken part in that great enterprise of which he must also have heard, in the so-called 'Journey to the East,' or the League expedition, or whatever it was then described as by the public. Oh yes, he smiled ironically, he certainly remembered it. In his circle of friends, this singular episode was mostly called, perhaps somewhat disrespectfully, 'the Children's Crusade.' This movement was not taken quite seriously in his circle. It had indeed been compared with some kind of theosophical movement or brotherhood. Just the same, they had been very surprised at the periodic successes of the undertaking. They had read with due respect about the courageous journey through Upper Swabia, of the triumph at Bremgarten, of the surrender of the Tessin mountain village, and had at times wondered whether the movement would like to place itself at the service of a republican government. Then, to be sure, the matter apparently petered out. Several of the former leaders left the movement; indeed, in some way they seemed to be ashamed of it and no longer wished to remember it. News about it came through very sparingly and it was always strangely contradictory, and so the whole matter was just placed aside *ad acta* and forgotten like so many eccentric political, religious or artistic movements of those post-war years. At that time so many prophets sprang up, so many secret societies with Messianic hopes appeared and then disappeared again leaving no trace.

His point of view was clear, it was that of a well-meaning sceptic. All others who had heard its story, but had not themselves taken part in it, probably thought the same about the League and the Journey to the East. It was not for me to convert Lukas, but I gave him some corrected information; for instance, that our League was in no way an off-shoot of the post-war years, but that it had extended throughout the whole of world history, sometimes certainly under the surface, but in an unbroken line, that even certain phases of the Great War were nothing else but stages in the history of our League; further, that Zoroaster, Lao Tse, Plato, Xenophon, Pythagoras, Albertus Magnus, Don Quixote, Tristram Shandy, Novalis and Baudelaire were co-founders and brothers of our League. He smiled exactly in the way that I expected.

'Well,' I said, 'I have not come here to instruct you, but to learn from you. It is my passionate desire to write, perhaps not a history of the League (even a whole army of well-equipped scholars would not be in a position to do this), but to tell quite simply the story of our journey. But I am quite unsuccessful in even approaching the subject. It is not a question of literary ability; I think I have this. Moreover, I have no ambitions in this respect. No, it is because the reality that I once experienced, together with my comrades, exists no longer, and although its memories are the most precious and vivid ones that I possess, they seem so far away, they are composed of such a different kind of fabric, that it seems as if they originated on other stars in other millennia, or as if they were hallucinations.'

'I can understand that!' cried Lukas eagerly. Our conversation was only just beginning to interest him. 'How well do I understand! That is just how I was affected by my war experiences. I thought I had experienced them clearly and vividly, I was almost bursting with images of them; the roll of film in my head seemed miles long. But when I sat at my writing-desk, on a chair, by a table, the razed villages and woods, the earth tremors caused by heavy bombardment, the conglomeration of filth and greatness, of fear and heroism, of mangled stomachs and heads, of fear of death and grim humour, were all immeasurably remote, only a dream, were not related to anything and could not really be conceived. You know that despite this, I finally wrote my war-book and that it is now read and discussed a great deal. But do you know, I do not think that ten books like it, each one ten times better and more vivid than mine, could convey any real picture of the war to the most serious reader, if he had not himself experienced the war. And there were not so many who had. Even those who took part in it did not for a long time experience it. And if many really did so – they forgot about it again. Next to the hunger to experience a thing, men have perhaps no stronger hunger than to forget.'

He was silent and looked perplexed and lost in

thought. His words had confirmed my own experiences and thoughts.

After a time I asked him warily, 'Then how was it possible for you to write the book?'

He thought for a moment, brought back from his reflections. 'It was only possible for me to do it,' he said, 'because it was necessary. I either had to write the book or be reduced to despair; it was the only means of saving me from nothingness, chaos and suicide. The book was written under this pressure and brought me the expected cure, simply because it was written, irrespective of whether it was good or bad. That was the only thing that counted. And whilst writing it, there was no need for me to think at all of any other reader but myself, or at the most, here and there another close war-comrade, and I certainly never thought then about the survivors, but always about those who fell in the war. Whilst writing it, I was as if delirious or crazy, surrounded by three or four people with mutilated bodies – that is how the book was produced.'

And suddenly he said – it was the end of our first conversation: 'Forgive me, I cannot say any more about it, not a single word more. I cannot, I will not. Good-bye.'

He pushed me out.

At our second meeting he was again calm and collected, had the same ironical smile and yet seemed to treat my problem seriously and to understand it fully. He made a few suggestions which seemed, however, of little use to me. At the end of the second and last conversation, he said to me almost casually:

'Listen, you continually come back to the episode with

the servant Leo. I don't like it; it seems to be an obstacle in your way. Free yourself, throw Leo overboard; he seems to be becoming a fixed idea.'

I wanted to reply that one could not write any books without fixed ideas. Instead he startled me with the quite unexpected question: 'Was he really called Leo?'

There was perspiration on my brow.

'Yes,' I said, 'of course he was called Leo.'

'Was that his Christian name?'

I stammered.

'No, his Christian name was – was – I don't know it any more. I have forgotten it. Leo was his surname. That was what everyone called him.'

While I was still speaking, Lukas had seized a thick book from his writing-desk and was turning over the leaves. With amazing speed he found and put his finger on a place on an open page in the book. It was a directory, and where his finger lay stood the name Leo.

'Look,' he laughed, 'we already have a Leo. Andreas Leo, 69a Seilergraben. It is an unusual name; perhaps this man knows something about your Leo. Go and see him; perhaps he can tell you what you want to know. I don't know. Forgive me, my time is limited. I am very pleased to have seen you.'

I reeled with stupefaction and excitement as I closed his door behind me. He was right. I could get nothing more from him.

On the very same day I went to Seilergraben, looked for the house and enquired about Mr. Andreas Leo. He lived in a room on the third floor. He was sometimes at home on

Sundays and in the evenings; during the day he went to work. I enquired about his occupation. He did this, that and the other, they said; he could do manicures, chiropody and massage; he also made ointments and herbal cures. In bad times, when there was little to do, he sometimes also occupied himself by training and trimming dogs. I went away and decided it was better not to visit this man, or, at any rate, not to tell him of my intentions. Nevertheless, I was very curious to see him. I therefore watched the house in the next few days during my frequent walks, and I shall also go there today, for up till now I have not been successful in meeting Andreas Leo face to face.

Oh, the whole business is driving me to despair, and yet it makes me happy, or rather excited and eager. It gives importance to myself and my life again, and that had been very much lacking.

It is possible that the practitioners and psychologists who attribute all human action to egoistic desires are right; I cannot indeed see that a man who serves a cause all his life, who neglects his pleasures and well-being, and sacrifices himself for some particular thing, really acts in the same way as a man who traffics in slaves or deals in munitions and squanders the proceeds on a life of pleasure. But no doubt I should immediately get the worst of it and be beaten in an argument with such a psychologist, for psychologists are, of course, people who always win. As far as I am concerned, they may be right. Then everything else that I have considered good and fine, and for which I have made sacrifices, has only been my egoistic desires. Indeed, every day I see my egoism more clearly in my plan to write some kind of history of the Journey to the East. At the beginning, it seemed to me that I was undertaking a laborious task in the name of a noble cause, but I see more and more that in the description of my journey I am only aiming at the same thing as Mr. Lukas with his war-book; namely, at saving my life by giving it meaning again.

If I could only see the way! If I could only make one step forward.

'Throw Leo overboard, free yourself from Leo!' Lukas said to me. I could just as much throw my head or my stomach overboard to get rid of them!

Dear God, help me a little.

Four

Now everything seems different again, and I do not yet know whether it has helped me in my problem or not. But I have had an experience, something has happened to me which I never expected – or no, did I not really expect it, did I not anticipate, hope for and really fear it? Yes, I did. Yet it remains strange and improbable enough.

I went to Seilergraben frequently, twenty times or more, at what I thought were favourable times, and often wandered past No. 69a, always with the thought, 'I shall try once more, and if there is nothing in it I shall not come again.' Yet I went again and again, and the day before yesterday my wish was fulfilled. Oh, and what a fulfilment it was!

As I approached the house of which I now knew every crack and fissure in its grey-green plaster, I heard the tune whistled of a little song or dance, a popular tune, coming from the upper window. I did not know anything yet, but I listened. The tune stirred my memory and some dormant recollections came to the fore. The music was banal but the whistling was wonderfully sweet, with soft and pleasing notes, unusually pure, as happy and as natural as the songs of birds. I stood and listened, enchanted, and at the same time strangely moved without, however, having any kind of accompanying thoughts. Or if I did, it was perhaps that it must be a very happy and amiable man who could whistle like that. For several minutes I stood there rooted to the spot and listened. An old man with a sick, sunken face went by. He saw me standing and listened too, just for a moment, then smiled at me with understanding as he went on. His beautiful, far-seeing old man's look seemed to say: 'You stay there, one does not hear whistling like that every day.' The old man's glance cheered me. I was sorry when he went past. At the same moment, however, I immediately realised that this whistling was the fulfilment of all my wishes, that the whistler must be Leo.

It was growing dark but there was still no light in any window. The tune, with its simple variations, was finished. There was silence. 'He will put the light on now,' I thought, but everything remained in darkness. Then I heard a door being opened upstairs and soon I also heard footsteps on the stairs. The door of the house was opened and someone came out, and his walk was like his whistling, light and jolly, but steady, healthy and youthful. It was a very slim, hatless man, not very tall, who walked there, and now my feeling was changed to certainty. It was Leo; not only the Leo from the directory, it was Leo himself, our dear travelling companion and servant Leo, whose disappearance ten or more years ago had brought us so much sadness and confusion. I nearly addressed him in the moment of my initial joy and surprise. Then I remembered that I had also often heard him whistling during the journey to the East. They were the same strains of previous times, and yet how strangely different they sounded to me! A feeling of sadness came over me like a stab in the heart: oh, how different everything had become since then, the sky, the air, the seasons, dreams, sleep, day and night! How greatly and terribly everything had changed for me when, through memory of the past alone, a whistle and the rhythm of a known step could affect me so deeply and give me so much pleasure and pain!

The man went close by me, his bare head, supple and serene on his bare neck, appeared above his blue open-neck shirt. The figure moved easily and gaily along the darkening lane, hardly audible in thin sandals or gym shoes. I followed him without any particular intention. How could I help but follow him! He walked down the lane, and although his step was light, effortless and youthful, it was also in keeping with the evening; it was of the same quality as the twilight, it was friendly and at one with the hour, with the subdued sounds from the centre of the town, with the half-light of the first lamps which were just beginning to appear.

He turned into the small park at St. Paul's Gate, disappeared amongst the tall round bushes, and I hurried so that I should not lose him. There he was again; he was sauntering slowly alongside the lilac bushes and the acacia. The path divided into two through the little wood. There were a couple of benches at the edge of the grass. Here under the trees it was already dark. Leo went past the first bench; a pair of lovers were sitting on it. The next bench was empty. He sat down, leaned against the bench, pressed his head back and for a time looked up at the leaves and the clouds. Then he took a small round white metal box out of his coat pocket, put it by his side on the bench, unscrewed the lid and slowly began to take something out of the box which he put into his mouth and ate with enjoyment. Meantime I walked to and from the entrance to the wood; I then went up to his bench and sat down at the other end. He looked up, gazed at me with clear grey eyes and went on eating. He was eating dried fruits, a few prunes and half apricots. He took them one after the other between two fingers, pressed and fingered each one a little, put them in his mouth and chewed them for a long time with enjoyment. It took a long time before he came to the last one and ate it. He then closed the box again and put it away, leaned back and stretched out his legs. I now saw that his cloth shoes had soles of plaited rope.

'It will rain tonight,' he said suddenly, I knew not whether to me or to himself.

'Yes, it looks like it,' I said, somewhat embarrassed, for as he had not yet recognised my figure and walk, it was possible and I was almost certain that he would now recognise me by my voice.

But no, he did not recognise me at all, not even by my voice, and although that had been my first wish, it nevertheless gave me a feeling of great disappointment. He did not recognise me. While he had remained the same after ten years and had apparently not aged at all, it was quite different with me, sadly different.

'You whistle very well,' I said. 'I heard you earlier on in Seilergraben. It gave me very much pleasure. I used to be a musician.'

'Oh, were you!' he said in a friendly manner. 'That is a great profession. Have you given it up, then?'

'Yes, for the time being. I have even sold my violin.'

'Have you? What a pity! Are you in difficulties – that is

to say, are you hungry? There is still some food at my house. I also have a little money in my purse.'

'Oh, no,' I said quickly, 'I did not mean that. I am in quite good circumstances. I have more than I need. But thank you very much; it was very kind of you to make the offer. One does not often meet such kind people.'

'Don't you think so? Well, maybe! People are often very strange. You are a strange person, too.'

'Am I? Why?'

'Well, because you have enough money and yet you sell your violin. Do you not, then, like music any more?'

'Oh, yes, but it sometimes happens that a man no longer finds pleasure in something that he previously loved. It sometimes happens that a man sells his violin or throws it to the wall, or that a painter one day burns all his pictures. Have you never heard of such a thing?'

'Oh, yes. That comes from despair. That does happen. I even knew two people who committed suicide. People like that are stupid and can be dangerous. One just cannot help some people. But what do you do now that you no longer have your violin?'

'Oh, this and that. I do not really do much. I am no longer young and I am also often ill. But why do you keep on talking about this violin? It is not really so important.'

'The violin? It made me think of King David.'

'King David? What has he to do with it?'

'He was also a musician. When he was quite young he used to play to King Saul and sometimes dispelled his bad moods with music. Later he became a king himself, a great king full of cares, having all sorts of moods and vexations. He wore a crown and conducted wars and all that kind of thing, and he also did many really wicked things and became very famous. But when I think of his life, the most beautiful part of it all is about the young David with his harp playing music to poor Saul, and it seems a pity to me that he later became a king. He was a much happier and better person when he was a musician.'

'Of course he was!' I exclaimed passionately. 'Of course, he was younger then, more handsome and happier. But one does not always remain young; your David would in time have grown older and uglier and would have been full of cares even if he had remained a musician. So he became the great David, performed his deeds and composed his psalms. Life is not just a game!'

Leo then rose and bowed. 'It is growing dark,' he said, 'and it will rain soon. I do not know a great deal more about the deeds that David performed, and whether they were really great. To be quite frank, I do not know very much more about his psalms either, but I should not like to say anything against them. But no account of David can prove to me that life is not just a game. That is just what life is when it is beautiful and happy – a game! Naturally, one can also do all kinds of other things with it, make a duty of it, or a battleground, or a prison, but that does not make it any prettier. Good-bye, pleased to have met you!'

This strange, lovable man began to move away in his light, steady and pleasing gait, and was on the point of disappearing when all my restraint and self-control broke down. I ran after him in despair and cried imploringly. 'Leo! Leo! You are Leo, aren't you? Do you not know me any more? We were League brothers together and should still be so. We were both travellers on the journey to the East. Have you really forgotten me, Leo? Do you really no longer remember the Crown Watchers, Klingsor and Goldmund, the Festival in Bremgarten and the gorge at Morbio Inferiore? Leo, have pity on me!'

He did not run away as I had feared but he also did not turn round; he walked steadily on as if he had heard nothing but gave me time to catch up to him, and did not seem to object to my joining him.

'You are so troubled and hasty,' he said kindly, 'that is not a good thing. It distorts the face and makes one ill. We shall walk quite slowly – it is so soothing. The few drops of rain are wonderful, aren't they? They come from the air like Eau de Cologne.'

'Leo,' I pleaded, 'have pity! Tell me just one thing; do you know me yet?'

'Ah,' he said kindly, and went on speaking as if to a sick or drunken man, 'you will be better now; it was only excitement. You ask if I know you. Well, which person really knows another or even himself? As for me, I am not one who understands people at all. I am not interested in them. Now, I understand dogs quite well, and also birds and cats – but I don't really know you, sir.'

'But do you not belong to the League? Did you not come on the journey with us?'

'I am still on the journey sir, and I still belong to the

League. So many come and go; one knows people and yet does not know them. It is much easier with dogs. Wait, stay here a moment!'

He raised a warning finger. We stood on the darkening garden path which was becoming increasingly enveloped in a thin descending dampness. Leo pursed up his lips and sent out a long, vibrating, soft whistle, waited a while and whistled again. I drew back a little as, suddenly, close to us, behind the trellis-work railing at which we stood, a large Alsatian dog jumped out of the bushes and, whining with pleasure, pressed close to the fence in order to be stroked by Leo's fingers between the bars and wires. The powerful animal's eyes gleamed a light green, and whenever his glance rested on me he growled deep down in his throat. It was like distant thunder, hardly audible.

'This is the Alsatian dog, Necker,' said Leo, introducing me. 'We are very good friends. Necker, here is a former violinist. You must not do anything to him, not even bark at him.'

We stood there, and Leo gently scratched the dog's damp coat through the railing. It really was a pretty scene; it pleased me very much to see how friendly he was with the dog and the pleasure that this nocturnal greeting gave him. At the same time, it was painful to me and seemed hardly bearable that Leo should be so friendly with this Alsatian, and probably with many, perhaps with all the dogs in the district, while a world of aloofness separated him from me. The friendship and intimacy which I beseechingly and humbly sought seemed not only to belong to this dog Necker, but to every animal, to every raindrop,

to every spot of ground on which Leo trod. He seemed to
dedicate himself steadfastly and to rest continually in an
easy, balanced relationship with his surroundings, knowing
all things, known and beloved by all. Only with me, who
loved and needed him so much, was there no contact,
only from me did he dissociate himself; he regarded me in
an unfriendly and cool fashion, was distant with me and
had erased me from his memory.

We walked slowly on. On the other side of the railing
the Alsatian accompanied him, making soft, contented
sounds of affection and pleasure, but without forgetting
my undesirable presence, for several times he suppressed
his growling tone of defence and hostility for Leo's sake.

'Forgive me,' I began again, 'I am attaching myself to
you and taking up your time. Naturally, you want to go
home and go to bed.'

'Not at all,' he said with a smile. 'I do not mind strolling
along throughout the night like this. I am not lacking in
either the time or the desire if it is not too much for you.'

He said this in a very friendly manner and certainly
without reservation. But he had hardly uttered the words
when I suddenly felt in my head and in every muscle of
my body how terribly tired I was, and how fatiguing every
step of this futile and embarrassing nocturnal wandering
was to me.

'I am really very tired,' I said dejectedly, 'I have only
just realised it. There is also no sense in wandering about
all night in the rain and being a nuisance to other people.'

'As you wish,' he said politely.

'Oh, Mr. Leo, you did not talk to me like that during the League's journey to the East. Have you really forgotten all about it? Oh, well, it is no use. Do not let me keep you any longer. Good night.'

He disappeared quickly into the dark night. I remained alone, foolish, with my head bent. I had lost the game. He did not know me; he did not want to know me; he made fun of me.

I went back along the path; the dog Necker barked angrily behind the railing. I shivered from weariness, grief and loneliness in the damp warmth of the summer night.

I had experienced similar hours in the past. During such periods of despair it seemed to me as if I, a lost pilgrim, had reached the extreme edge of the world, and there was nothing left for me to do but to satisfy my last desire: to let myself fall from the edge of the world into the void – to death. In the course of time this despair returned many times; the compelling suicidal impulse, however, had been diverted and had almost vanished. Death was no longer nothingness, a void, negation. It had also become many other things to me. I now accepted the hours of despair as one accepts acute physical pain; one endures it, complainingly or defiantly; one feels it swell and increase, and sometimes there is a raging or mocking curiosity as to how much further it can go, to what extent the pain can still increase.

All the disgust for my disillusioned life which, since my return from the unsuccessful journey to the East, had become increasingly worthless and spiritless, all disbelief in myself and my abilities, all envious and regretful longing for the good and great times which I had once experienced, grew like a pain within me, grew as high as a tree, like a mountain, tugged at me, and was all related to the former task that I had begun, to the account of the Journey to the East and the League. It now seemed to me that even its accomplishment was no longer desirable or worthwhile. Only one hope still seemed worthwhile to me – to cleanse and redeem myself to some extent through my work, through my service to the memory of that great time, to bring myself once again into contact with the League and its experiences.

When I reached home I turned on the light, sat down at my desk in my wet clothes, my hat on my head, and wrote a letter. I wrote ten, twelve, twenty pages of grievances, remorse and entreaty to Leo. I described my need to him, conjured up images of our common experiences, of our former mutual friends. I bewailed the endless extreme difficulties which had shattered my noble enterprise. The weariness of the moment had disappeared; excited, I sat there and wrote. Despite all difficulties, I wrote, I would endure the worst possible thing rather than divulge a single secret of the League. Despite everything, I would not fail to complete my work in memory of the Journey to the East, in glorification of the League. As if in a fever, I covered page after page with hastily written words. The grievances, indictments and self-accusations tumbled from me like water from a breaking jug, without reflection, without faith, without hope of reply, only with the desire to unburden myself. While it was yet night I took the thick, confused letter to the nearest letter-box. Then, at last, it was nearly morning. I turned out the light, went to the small attic-bedroom next to my living-room and went to bed. I feel asleep immediately and slept very deeply and for a long time.

Five

After awakening and dozing off again several times, I awoke the following day with a headache but feeling rested. To my extreme astonishment, pleasure and also embarrassment, I found Leo in the living-room. He was sitting on the edge of a chair and looked as if he had been waiting a long time.

'Leo,' I cried, 'you have come!'

'They have sent me for you from the League,' he said. 'You wrote me a letter in connection with it. I gave it to the officials. You are to appear before the High Throne. Can we go?'

In confusion I hastened to put on my shoes. The desk, disarranged the previous night, still had a somewhat disturbed and disorderly appearance. For the moment I hardly knew any more what I had written there so forcibly and full of anguish a few hours ago. Still, it did not seem to have been in vain. Something had happened. Leo had come.

Suddenly, for the first time, I realised the significance of his words. So there was still a 'League' of which I no longer knew anything, which existed without me and which no longer considered me as belonging to it! There was still a League and the High Throne! There were still the officials; they had sent for me! I went hot and cold at the realisation. I had lived in this town many months, occupied with my notes about the League and our journey and did not know whether the rest of the League still existed, where it was, and whether I was perhaps its last member. Indeed, to be quite frank, at certain times I was not sure whether the League and my membership of it had ever been real. And now Leo stood there, sent by the League to fetch me. I was remembered, I was summoned, they wanted to listen to me, perhaps to pass judgment on me. Good! I was ready. I was ready to show that I had not been unfaithful to the League. I was ready to obey. Whether the officials punished me or pardoned me, I was ready in advance to accept everything, to agree with their judgment in everything and to be obedient to them.

We set off. Leo went on ahead, and again, as I did many years ago when I watched him and the way he walked, I had to admire him as a good and perfect servant. He walked along the lanes in front of me, nimbly and patiently, in- dicating the way: he was the perfect guide, the perfect servant at his task, the perfect official. Yet he put my patience to no small test. The League had summoned me, I was awaited by the High Throne, everything was at stake for me: the whole of my future life would be decided, the whole of my past life would now either retain or completely lose its meaning – I trembled with expectation, pleasure, anxiety and suppressed fear. And so the route that Leo took seemed, in my impatience, intolerably long, for I had to follow my guide for more than two hours by way of the strangest and seemingly most capricious détours. Leo kept me waiting twice in front of a church in which he went to pray. For a long time that seemed endless to me, he remained meditating and absorbed in front of the old townhall, and told me about its foundation in the fifteenth century by a famous member of the League. And although the way he took this walk seemed so painstaking, zealous and purposeful, I became quite confused by the détours, roundabouts and zig-zags by which he approached his goal. The walk, which took us all morning, could easily have been done in a quarter of an hour.

At last he led me into a sleepy, suburban lane, and into a very large, silent building. Outside it looked like an extended Council building or a museum. At first there was not a soul to be seen anywhere. Corridors and stairs were deserted and echoed to our footsteps. Leo began to search among the passages, stairs and antechambers. Once, he cautiously opened a big door, on the other side of which we saw a crowded artist's studio; in front of an easel stood the artist Klingsor in his shirt-sleeves – oh, how many years was it since I had seen his beloved face! But I did not dare to greet him; the time was not that ripe for that. I was expected. I had been summoned. Klingsor did not pay very much attention to us. He nodded to Leo; either he did not see me or did not recognise me, and silently indicated to us in a friendly but decisive way to go out, not tolerating any interruption of his work.

Finally, at the top of the immense building, we arrived at a garret-storey, which smelled of paper and cardboard, and all along the walls for many hundreds of yards protruded cupboard-doors, backs of books and bundles of documents; a gigantic archive, a vast chancery. Nobody took any notice of us; everyone was silently occupied. It seemed to me as if the whole world, including the starry heavens, was governed or at least recorded and observed from there. For a long time we stood there and waited; many archive and library officials hastened around us silently with catalogue dockets and numbers in their hands. Ladders were placed in position and mounted, lifts and small trucks were carefully and quietly set into motion. Finally, Leo began to sing. I listened to the tune, deeply moved; it had once been very familiar to me. It was the melody of one of our League songs.

At the sound of the song, everything immediately sprang into movement. The officials drew back, the hall extended into dusky remoteness. The industrious people, small and unreal, worked in the gigantic archive region in the background. The foreground, however, was spacious and empty. The hall extended to an impressive length. In the middle, arranged in strict order, there were many benches, and partly from the background and partly out of the numerous doors came many officials who slowly approached the benches and one by one sat down on them. One row of benches after the other was slowly filled. The structure of benches gradually rose and culminated in a high throne, which was not yet occupied. The solemn Synedrium was crowded right up to the throne. Leo looked at me with a warning glance to be patient, silent and respectful, and disappeared amongst the crowd; all of a sudden he was gone and I could no longer see him. But here and there amidst the officials who assembled around the High Throne I perceived familiar faces, serious or smiling. I saw the figure of Albertus Magnus, the ferryman Vasudeva, the artist Klingsor, and others.

At last it became quiet and the Speaker stepped forward. Small and alone I stood before the High Throne, prepared for everything, in a state of great anxiety, but also in full accord with what would take place and be resolved here.

Clearly and evenly the Speaker's voice rang through the hall. 'Self-accusation of a deserter League brother,' I heard him announce. My knees trembled. It was a question of my life. But it was right that it should be so; everything must now be put in order. The Speaker continued.

'Is your name H.H.? Did you join in the march through Upper Swabia, and in the festival at Bremgarten? Did you desert your colours shortly after Morbio Inferiore? Did you confess that you wanted to write a story of the Journey to the East? Did you consider yourself hampered by your vow of silence about the League's secrets?'

I answered question after question with 'Yes,' even those which were incomprehensible and terrifying to me.

The officials conferred in whispers and with gestures for a short time; then the Speaker stepped forward again and announced:

'The self-accuser is herewith empowered to reveal publicly every law and secret of the League which is known to him. Moreover, the whole of the League's archives are placed at his disposal for his work.'

The Speaker drew back. The officials disbanded and again slowly disappeared, some into the background of the hall and some through the exits; there was complete silence in the large hall. I was looking anxiously around me when I saw something lying on one of the chancery documents which seemed familiar to me. When I picked it up, I recognized my work, my delicate offspring, the manuscript I had begun. *The Story of the Journey to the East,* by H.H., was inscribed on the blue envelope. I seized it and read the small, close, hand-written, oft-times crossed out and corrected pages. In haste, eager to work, I was overwhelmed with the feeling that now at last, with approval from higher quarters, indeed assistance, I was to be allowed to complete my task. When I considered that no vow any longer bound me, that I had access to the archives, to those immense treasure-chambers, my task seemed to me greater and more worth-while than ever.

However, the more pages I read of my handwriting, the less did I like the manuscript. Even in my former most despondent hours it had never seemed so futile and absurd to me as now. Everything seemed so confused and stupid; the clearest relationships were distorted, the most obvious were forgotten, the trivial and the unimportant pushed into the foreground. It must be written again, right from the beginning. As I continued reading the manuscript, I had to cross out sentence after sentence, and as I crossed them out, they crumbled up on the paper, and the clear, sloping letters separated into assorted fragments, into strokes and points, into circles, small flowers and stars, and the pages were covered like carpets with graceful, meaningless, ornamental designs. Soon there was nothing more left of my text; on the other hand, there was much unused paper left for my work. I pulled myself together. I tried to see things clearly. Naturally I had been unable to give a clear, impartial account before, for everything was in fact concerned with secrets which I was forbidden to reveal by my oath to the League. I had tried to avoid an objective presentation of the story, and without regard to the more important relationships, aims and purposes, I had simply restricted myself to my personal experiences. But one could see where that had led. On the other hand, there was no longer a pledge of silence and no more restrictions. I was given complete official permission, and, moreover, the whole of the inexhaustible archives lay open to me.

It was clear to me that even if my former work had not broken up into ornamentation, I had to begin the whole thing afresh, with a new foundation, and build it up again. I decided to begin with a short account of the League, its foundation and constitution. The extensive, endless, gigantic labelled catalogues on all the tables, which reached far into the distance and semi-darkness, must surely give an answer to all my questions.

First of all I decided to examine the archives at random. I had to learn how to use this tremendous machine. Naturally, I looked for the League document before anything else.

'League document,' it stated in the catalogue, 'see section Chrysostomos, group V, verse 39, 8.' Right. I found the section, the group and the verse quite easily. The archives were wonderfully arranged. And now I held the League document in my hand. I had to be prepared for the possibility that I might not be able to read it. As a matter of fact, I could not read it. It was written in Greek characters, it seemed to me, and I understood a certain amount of Greek, but for one thing it was in extremely ancient, strange writing, the characters of which, despite apparent clarity, were for the most part illegible to me, and, for another thing, the text was written in dialect or in a secret symbolical language, of which I only occasionally understood a word as if from a distance, by sound and analogy. But I was not yet discouraged. Even if the document remained unreadable, its characters brought back to me vivid memories of the past. In particular, I clearly saw my friend Longus writing Greek and Hebrew characters in the garden in the evening, the characters changing into birds, dragons and snakes in the night.

Looking through the catalogue, I trembled at the abundance of material that awaited me there. I came across many familiar words and many well-known names. With a start, I came across my own name, but I did not dare to consult the archives about it – who could bear to hear the verdict of an omniscient Court of Law on oneself? On the other hand, I found, for example, the name of the artist Paul Klee, whose acquaintance I had made during the journey and who was a friend of Klingsor's. I looked up his number in the archives. I found there a small gold-plated dish on which a clover was either painted or engraved. The first of its three leaves represented a small blue sailing-boat, the second a fish with coloured scales and the third book like a telegram-form on which was written:

> As blue as snow,
> Is Paul like Klee.*

It also gave me a melancholy pleasure to read about

*Klee = clover.

Klingsor, Longus, Max and Tilli. Also I could not resist the desire to learn something more about Leo. On Leo's catalogue label was written:

Cave!
   Archiepisc. XIX. Diacon. D. VII.
    Corno Ammon. 6
     Cave!

The two 'Cave' warnings impressed me. I could not bring myself to penetrate this secret. However, with every new attempt, I began to realise more and more what an undreamt-of abundance of material, knowledge and magic formulæ these archives contained. It included, it seemed to me, the whole world.

After happy or bewildering excursions into many branches of knowledge, I returned several times to the label 'Leo' with ever-increasing curiosity. Each time the double 'Cave' deterred me. Then, while going through another filing cabinet, I came across the word 'Fatima,' with the notes:

       princ. orient. 2
        noct. mill. 983
         hort. delic. 07

I looked for and found the place in the archives. There lay a tiny locket which could be opened and contained a miniature portrait of a ravishingly beautiful princess, which in an instant reminded me of all the thousand and one nights, of all the tales of my youth, of all the dreams and wishes of that great period when, in order to travel to

Fatima in the Orient, I had served my novitiate and had reported myself as a member of the League. The locket was wrapped in a finely-spun mauve silk kerchief, which had an immeasurably remote and sweet fragrance, reminiscent of princesses and the East. As I breathed in this remote, rare, magic fragrance, I was suddenly and powerfully overwhelmed with the realisation of the sweet magic which had enveloped me when I commenced my pilgrimage to the East, and how the pilgrimage was shattered by treacherous and, in fact, unknown obstacles, how the magic had then vanished more and more, and what desolation, disillusionment and barren despair had since been my life's breath, my food and drink! I could no longer see the kerchief or the portrait, so thick was the veil of tears which covered my eyes. Ah, now, I thought, the portrait of the Arabian princess could no longer suffice to act as a charm against the world and hell, and make me into a knight and crusader; I would now need other stronger charms. But how sweet, how innocent, how blissful had been that dream which had haunted my youth, which had made me a story-teller, a musician and a novitiate, and had led me to Morbio!

Sounds awakened me from my meditation. From all sides the unending spaciousness of the archive chamber confronted me eerily. A new thought, a new pain shot through me like a flash of lightning. I, in my simplicity, wanted to write the story of the League, I, who could not decipher or understand one-thousandth part of those millions of scripts, books, pictures and references in the archives! Humbled, unspeakably foolish, unspeakably ridiculous, not understanding myself, feeling extremely small, I saw myself standing in the middle of everything that I had been allowed to amuse myself with, so that I might realise exactly what the League, and I myself, was.

The officials came through the numerous doors in enormous numbers. I could still recognise many of them through my tears. I recognised Jup, the magician, I recognised Lindhorst, the archivist, I recognised Mozart dressed as Pablo. The illustrious assembly filled the many rows of seats, which became higher and narrower at the back; over the throne which formed the top, I saw a shining golden canopy.

The Speaker stepped forward and announced: 'The League is ready to pass judgment, through its officials, on the self-accuser H., who felt bound to keep silent about League secrets, and who has now realised how strange and blasphemous was his intention to write the story of a journey to which he was not equal, and an account of a League in whose existence he no longer believed and to which he had become unfaithful.'

He turned towards me and said in his clear, proclamatory voice: 'Self-accuser H., do you agree to recognize the Court of Justice and to submit to its judgment?'

'Yes,' I replied.

'Self-accuser H.,' he continued, 'do you agree that the Court of Justice of the officials pass judgment on you without the President in the Chair, or do you desire the President himself to pass judgment on you?'

'I agree,' I said, 'to be judged by the officials, either with or without the President in the Chair.'

The Speaker was about to reply when, from the very back of the hall, a soft voice said: 'The President is ready to pass judgment himself.'

The sound of this soft voice shook me strangely. Right from the depths of the room, from the remote horizons of the archives, came a man. His walk was light and peaceful, his robe sparkled with gold. He came nearer amid the silence of the assembly, and I recognized his walk, I recognized his movements, and finally I recognized his face. It was Leo. In a magnificent, festive robe, he climbed through the rows of officials to the High Throne like a Pope. Like a magnificent, rare flower, he carried the brilliance of his attire up the stairs. Each row of officials rose to greet him as he passed. He bore his radiant office conscientiously, humbly, dutifully, as humbly as a holy Pope or patriarch bears his insignia.

I was deeply intrigued and moved in anticipation of the judgment which I was humbly prepared to accept, whether it would now bring punishment or grace. I was no less deeply moved and amazed that it was Leo, the former porter and servant, who now stood at the head of the whole League and was ready to pass judgment on me. But I was still more stirred, amazed, startled and happy at the great discovery of the day: that the League was as completely stable and mighty as ever, that it was not Leo and the League who had deserted and disillusioned me, but only I who had been so weak and foolish as to misinterpret my own experiences, to doubt the League, to consider the Journey to the East a failure, and to regard myself as the survivor and chronicler of a concluded and forgotten tale, while I was nothing more than a runaway, a traitor, a deserter. Amazement and joy lay in this recognition. I stood there, small and humble, at the foot of the High Throne, from which I had once been accepted as a brother of the League, from which I had once undergone my novitiate ceremony, had received the League ring and had immediately been sent to the servant Leo on the journey. And in the middle of everything, I was aware of a new sin, a new inexplicable loss, a new shame: I no longer possessed the League ring. I had lost it, I did not know when or where, and I had not missed it once until this day!

Meantime, the President, the golden-clad Leo, began to speak in his beautiful, gentle voice; his words reached me gently and comfortingly, as gentle and comforting as sunshine.

'The self-accuser,' came the words from the High Throne 'has had the opportunity to rid himself of some of his errors. There is much to be said against him. It may be conceivable and very excusable that he was unfaithful to the League, that he reproached the League with his own failings and follies, that he doubted its continuation, that he had the strange ambition to become the historian of the League. All this does not weigh heavily against him. They are, if the self-accuser will permit me the phrase, only novitiate stupidities. They can be dismissed with a smile.'

I breathed deeply and a faint smile passed over the whole of the illustrious assembly. That the most serious of my sins, even my illusion that the League no longer existed and that I was the only disciple left, were only regarded by the President as 'stupidities,' as trifles, was a tremendous relief to me and at the same time sent me most definitely back to my starting-point.

'But,' continued Leo, and his gentle voice was now sad and serious – 'there are many more serious offences imputed to the defendant and the worst of them is that he does not stand as self-accuser for these sins, but appears to be unaware of them. He deeply regrets having wronged the League in thought; he cannot forgive himself for not recognising the President Leo in the servant Leo, and is on the point of realising the extent of his infidelity to the League. But while he took these sinful thoughts and follies all too seriously, and only just realises with relief that they can be dismissed with a smile, he stubbornly forgets his real offences, which are legion, each one of which is serious enough to warrant severe punishment.'

My heart beat quickly. Leo turned towards me. 'Defendant H., later you will have insight to your errors and you will also be shown how to avoid them in future. But just to show you what little understanding you still have of your position, I ask you: Do you remember your walk through the town accompanied by the servant Leo, who, as messenger, had to bring you before the High Throne? Yes, you remember. And do you remember how we passed the Town Hall, the Church of St. Paul and the Cathedral, and how the servant Leo entered the Cathedral in order to kneel and pray awhile, and how you not only refrained from entering with me to perform your devotions in accordance with the fourth precept of your League vow, but how you remained outside, impatient and bored, waiting for the end of the tedious ceremony which seemed so unnecessary

to you, which was nothing more to you than a disagreeable
test of your egoistic impatience? Yes, you remember. By
your behaviour at the Cathedral gate alone, you have already trampled on the fundamental requirements and
customs of the League. You have slighted religion, you
have been contemptuous towards a League brother, you
have impatiently rejected an opportunity and invitation to
prayer and meditation. These sins would be unforgivable
were there not special extenuating circumstances in your
case.'

He had now struck home. Everything would now be
said; there would be no more secondary issues, no more
mere stupidities. He was more than right. He had struck at
my heart.

'We do not want to count up all the defendant's errors,'
continued the President, 'he is not going to be judged
according to the letter, and we know that it only needed
our reminder to awaken the defendant's conscience and
make him a repentant self-accuser.

'Just the same, self-accuser H., I would advise you to
bring some of your other acts before the judgment of your
conscience. Must I remind you of the evening when you
visited the servant Leo and wished to be recognised by him
as a League brother, although this was impossible, for you
had made yourself unrecognisable as a League brother?
Must I remind you of things which you yourself said to the
servant Leo? About the sale of your violin? About the
dreadful, stupid, narrow, suicidal life which you have led
for years?

'There is still one more thing, League brother H., about

which I should not keep silent. It is quite possible that the servant Leo did you an injustice that evening. Let us suppose that he did. The servant Leo was perhaps too strict, perhaps too rational; perhaps he did not show enough forbearance and sympathy towards you and your circumstances. But there are higher authorities and more infallible judges than the servant Leo. What was the animal's judgment on you, defendant? Do you remember the dog Necker? Do you remember his rejection and condemnation of you? He is incorruptible, he does not take sides, he is not a League brother.'

He paused. Yes, the Alsatian Necker! He had certainly rejected me and condemned me. I agreed. Judgment was already passed on me by the Alsatian, already by myself.

'Self-accuser H.,' began Leo again, and from the golden gleam of his robes and canopy his voice now rang out cool and bright and clear, like the voice of the commandant when he appears before Don Giovanni's door in the last act. 'Self-accuser H., you have listened to me. You have agreed with me. You have, we presume, already passed judgment on yourself?'

'Yes,' I said in a soft voice, 'yes.'

'It is, we presume, an unfavourable judgment which you have passed on yourself?'

'Yes,' I whispered.

Leo then rose from the throne and gently stretched out his arms.

'I now turn to you, my officials. You have heard and know how things have been with League brother H. It is a lot that is not unfamiliar to you; many of you have had to experience it yourselves. The defendant did not know until this hour, or could not really believe, that his apostasy and aberration were a test. For a long time he did not give in. He endured it for many years, knowing nothing about the League, remaining alone, and seeing everything in which he believed in ruins. Finally, he could no longer hide and contain himself. His suffering became too great, and you know that as soon as suffering becomes acute enough, one goes forward. Brother H. was led to despair in his test, and despair is the result of each earnest attempt to understand and vindicate human life. Despair is the result of each earnest attempt to go through life with virtue, justice and understanding and to fulfil their requirements. Children live on one side of despair, the awakened on the other side. Defendant H. is no longer a child and is not yet fully awakened. He is still in the midst of despair. He will overcome it and thereby go through his second novitiate. We welcome him anew into the League, the meaning of which he no longer claims to understand. We give back to him his lost ring, which the servant Leo has kept for him.'

The Speaker then brought the ring, kissed me on the cheek and placed the ring on my finger. Hardly had I looked at the ring, hardly had I felt its metallic coolness on my fingers, when a thousand things occurred to me, a thousand inconceivable acts of neglect. Above all, it occurred to me that the ring had four stones at equal distances apart, and that it was a rule of the League and part of the vow to turn the ring slowly on the finger at least once a day, and at each of the four stones to bring to mind one of the four basic precepts of the vow. I had not only lost the ring and had not once missed it, but during all those dreadful years I had also no longer repeated the four basic precepts or thought of them. Immediately, I tried to say them again inwardly. I had an idea what they were, they were still within me, they belonged to me as does a name which one will remember in a moment but at that particular moment cannot be recalled. No, it remained silent within me, I could not repeat the rules, I had forgotten the wording. I had forgotten the rules; for many years I had not repeated them, for many years I had not observed them and held them sacred – and yet I had considered myself a loyal League brother.

The Speaker patted my arm kindly when he observed my dismay and deep shame. Then I heard the President speak again:

'Defendant and self-accuser H., you are acquitted, but I have to tell you that it is the duty of a brother who is acquitted in such a case to enter the ranks of the officials and occupy one of their seats as soon as he has passed a test of his faith and obedience. He has the option of choosing the test. Now, brother H., answer my questions!

'Are you prepared to tame a wild dog as a test of your faith?'

I drew back in horror.

'No, I could not do it,' I cried, moving away.

'Are you prepared and willing to burn the League's archives immediately at our command, as our Speaker burns a portion of them now before your eyes?'

The Speaker stepped forward, plunged his hands into the well-arranged filing-cabinets, drew out both hands full

of papers, many hundreds of papers, and to my horror
burnt them over a coal-pan.

'No,' I said, drawing back, 'I could not do that either.'

'*Cave, frater,*' cried the President. 'Take heed, impetuous
brother! I have begun with the easiest tasks which require
the smallest amount of faith. Each succeeding task will be
increasingly difficult. Answer me: are you prepared and
willing to consult our archives about yourself?'

I went cold and held my breath, but I had understood.
Each question would become more and more difficult;
there was no escape except into what was still worse.
Breathing deeply, I stood up and said yes.

The Speaker led me to the tables where the hundreds of
filing-cabinets stood. I looked for and found the letter H. I
found my name and, indeed, first of all that of my ancestor
Eoban, who, four hundred years ago, had also been a
member of the League. Then there was my own name, with
the comment:

Chattorum r. gest. XC.

civ. Calv. infid. 49.

The sheet shook in my hand. Meanwhile, the officials
rose from their seats one after the other, held out their
hands to me, looked me straight in the face, then went away.
The High Throne was vacated and, last of all, the President
descended the throne, held out his hand to me, looked me in
the face, smiled his pious, kind bishop's smile and left the
hall last of all. I remained there alone, the note in my hand
to refer to the archives for information.

I could not immediately bring myself to take the step of

consulting the archives about myself. I stood hesitating in the empty hall and saw extending for a long way the boxes, cupboards, pigeon-holes and cabinets, the accumulation of all the worth-while knowledge to which I could ever gain access. Yet as much from fear of seeing my own record sheet as from a burning desire for knowledge, I allowed my own affairs to wait a little in order to learn first about one thing and another which was important to me and my story of the Journey to the East. To be sure, I had long really known that my story had already been condemned and disposed of and that I should never finish writing it. Just the same, I was curious.

I noticed a badly-filed memorandum projecting from amongst the others in one of the filing-cabinets I went towards it and drew out the memorandum on which was written:

Morbio Inferiore.

No other catch-word could have expressed the extent of my curiosity more briefly and accurately. With my heart beating quickly, I looked up the place in the archives. It was a section of the archives which contained a rather large number of papers. On the top lay a copy of a description of the Morbio Gorge taken from an old Italian book, then there was a quarto sheet with short notes on the part which Morbio had played in the history of the League. All the notes referred to the Journey to the East and indeed to the base and group to which I had belonged. Our group, it was recorded here, had arrived at Morbio on its journey. There it was submitted to a test which it did not pass, namely, the disappearance of Leo. Although the League's rules should have guided us, and although even in the event of a League group remaining without a leader, the precepts held good and had been inculcated in us at the beginning of the journey, yet from the moment our whole group discovered the disappearance of Leo it had lost its head and faith, had entertained doubts and entered into futile arguments. In the end, the whole group, contrary to the spirit of the League, had broken up into factions and disbanded. This explanation of the disaster of Morbio could no longer surprise me much. On the other hand, I was extremely surprised at what I read further on about the breaking-up of our group, namely, that no less than three of our League brothers had made an attempt to write an account of our journey and had given a description of the events at Morbio. I was one of these three and a fair copy of my manuscript was included in the section. I read through the two others with the strangest feelings. Basically, both writers described the events of that day not very differently from the way I had done, and yet how different they seemed to me! I read in one of them:

'It was the absence of the servant Leo which revealed to us, suddenly and terribly, the extent of the dissention and the perplexities which shattered our hitherto apparent complete unity. A few of us, to be sure, immediately knew or suspected that Leo had neither come to any harm nor run away, but that he had secretly been recalled by the League officials. Yet not one of us can contemplate without feelings of deepest repentance and shame how badly we underwent this test. Hardly had Leo left us, when faith and concord amongst us was at an end; it was as if the life-blood of our group flowed away from an invisible wound. First there were differences of opinion, then open quarrels about the most futile and ridiculous questions. For example, I remember that our very popular and praiseworthy choir-master H.H. suddenly maintained that the missing Leo had also taken in his bag, along with other valuable objects, the ancient sacred document, the original manuscript of the Master. This statement was heatedly disputed for days. Treated symbolically, H.'s absurd assertion was really remarkably significant; indeed, it did seem as if the prosperity of the League, the cohesion of the whole, was completely gone with Leo's departure from our little group. The very same musician H. was a sad example of this. Until the day of Morbio Inferiore he was one of the most loyal and faithful League brothers, as well as popular as an artist, and, despite many weaknesses of character, he was one of our most active members. But he relapsed into brooding, depression and mistrust, became more than negligent in his duties, and began to be intolerant, nervous and quarrelsome. As he finally remained behind on the march one day and did not appear again, it did not occur to anyone to stop on his behalf and look for him; it was evidently a case of desertion. Unfortunately, he was not the only one, and finally nothing was left of our little travelling group. . . .'

I found this passage in the other historian's work:

'Just as ancient Rome collapsed after Cæsar's death, or democratic thought throughout the world on Wilson's desertion of the colours, so did our League break up on the unhappy day of Morbio. As far as blame and responsibility can be mentioned, two apparently harmless members were to blame for the collapse, the musician H.H. and Leo, one of the servants. These two men were previously popular and faithful members of the League, although lacking in understanding of its significance in world history. They disappeared one day without leaving any trace, taking with them many valuable possessions and important documents, which indicates that both wretches were bribed by enemies of the League....'

If the memory of this historian was so very confused and inaccurate, although he apparently made the report in all good faith and with the conviction of its complete veracity – what was the value of my own notes? If ten other accounts by other authors were found about Morbio, Leo and myself, they would presumably all contradict and censure each other. No, our historical efforts were of no use; there was no point in continuing with them and reading them; one could quietly let them be covered with dust in this section of the archives.

A shudder went through me at the thought of what I should still learn in this hour. How awry, altered and distorted everything and everyone was in these mirrors, how mockingly and unattainably did the face of truth hide itself behind all these reports, counter-reports and legends! What was still truth? What was still credible? And what would remain when I also learned about myself, about my own character and history from the knowledge stored in these archives?

I must be prepared for anything. Suddenly I could bear

the uncertainty and suspense no longer. I hastened to the section *Chattorum res gestæ*, looked for my sub-division and number and stood in front of the part marked with my name. This was a niche, and when I drew the thin curtains aside I saw that it contained nothing written. It contained nothing but a figure, an old and worn-looking model made from wood or wax, in pale colours. It appeared to be a kind of deity or barbaric idol. At first glance it was entirely incomprehensible to me. It was a figure that really consisted of two; it had a common back. I stared at it for a while, disappointed and surprised. Then I noticed a candle in a metal candlestick fixed to the wall of the niche. A match-box lay there. I lit the candle and the strange double figure was now brightly illuminated.

Only slowly did it dawn upon me. Only slowly and gradually did I begin to suspect and then perceive what it was intended to represent. It represented a figure which was myself, and this likeness of myself was unpleasantly weak and half-real; it had blurred features, and in its whole expression there was something unstable, weak, dying or wishing to die, and looked rather like a piece of sculpture which could be called 'Transitoriness' or 'Decay,' or something similar. On the other hand, the other figure which was joined to mine to make one, was strong in colour and form, and just as I began to realise whom it resembled, namely, the servant and President Leo, I discovered a second candle in the wall and lit this also. I now saw the double figure representing Leo and myself, not only becoming clearer and each image more alike, but I also saw that the surface of the figures was transparent and that one could look inside as one can look through the glass of a bottle or vase. Inside the figures I saw something moving, slowly, extremely slowly, in the same way that a snake moves which has fallen asleep. Something was taking place there, something like a very slow, smooth but continuous flowing or melting; indeed, something melted or poured across from my image to that of Leo's. I perceived that my image was in the process of adding to and flowing into Leo's, nourishing and strengthening it. It seemed that, in time, all the substance from one image would flow into the other and only one would remain: Leo. He must grow, I must disappear.

As I stood there and looked and tried to understand what I saw, I recalled a short conversation that I had once had with Leo during the festive days at Bremgarten. We had talked about the creations of poetry being more vivid and real than the poets themselves.

The candles burned low and went out. I was overcome by an infinite weariness and desire to sleep, and I turned away to find a place where I could lie down and sleep.

Other Panthers For Your Enjoyment

Some British

☐ Piers Paul Read   **THE JUNKERS**   30p
An exciting and important novel about love and danger in today's
divided Europe by one of Britain's finest young writers.
'Dazzling' – *Financial Times*. 'Compelling' – *The Observer*

☐ James Plunkett   **STRUMPET CITY**   50p
All big city life (Dublin is the city in the case of this wonderful
novel) is here – from saints (?) to sinners. The sinners need no
question mark – they're precisely what they're described as. A big
novel if ever there was one. Reviewers hailed it as the greatest novel
since DR. ZHIVAGO.

☐ Philip Callow   **THE BLISS BODY**   30p
Colin was young and wanted a woman – then he met Leila,
attractive, sexy, experienced. She was also married; which didn't
stop either of them. But there's always a price. *The Observer*
described the author as a 'confident successor to D. H. Lawrence'.

☐ Colin MacInnes   **WESTWARD TO
LAUGHTER**   30p
MacInnes sails westward in splendid style to murder, rape, piracy and
rebellion in the 17th century Caribbean. It's a novel that's got
something for everybody, and it 'takes the reader by storm' –
Spectator'

☐ Thomas Wiseman   **THE QUICK AND
THE DEAD**   40p
The Europe of the Nazis – from the ultra-sophisticated sexual
Viennese scene to the brutal battlefields of Yugoslavia. The
author's teeming characters are people corrupted beyond all
hope. *Time* Magazine wrote: 'An extraordinary novel . . .
Brilliant'. *The Observer*: 'Comedy and stark atrocity. Life crackles
on every page'.

☐ Simon Raven   **THE JUDAS BOY**   30p
Ambiguous sex, possible danger, final betrayal – Fielding Gray goes
to Greece on a TV fact-finding mission and is there seduced – quite
literally seduced – by a corrupt, golden boy who's the paid agent
of an American undercover man. 'Cynical and civilised' –
Evening Standard

Some Americans

☐ Gore Vidal   **WASHINGTON D. C.**   37p
A sour, fascinating look behind the scenes of the political capital
of the western world – who uses who, and how, and why . . . and
the lethal results.

☐ Edmund Wilson   **MEMOIRS OF**
                                    HECATE COUNTY   30p
The unexpurgated edition of a book that has become one of the
most controversial of the century. 'Very decidedly not for the
squeamish' – *The Times*

☐ James Jones   **SOME CAME**
                                    RUNNING   45p
By the author of FROM HERE TO ETERNITY.

☐ David Ely   **THE TOUR**   35p
American Intelligence arranges a package tour for the idle rich
which involves them in a secret and terrifying war game.

☐ Jock Carroll   **THE SHY**
                                    PHOTOGRAPHER   25p
The amorous adventures of Arthur King, a shy young candid
cameraman, in the busy world of film starlets and big business.

☐ Louis Auchincloss   **THE RECTOR OF**
                                    JUSTIN   45p
'Must be reckoned in the front rank of mid-century American
novels' – *Life*. 'Outstanding example of the novel as entertainment' –
Cyril Connolly. Dr. Prescott has a mania – to give his
long-established school a fame that has always eluded it. He succeeds,
only to make the very human discovery that obsessions have to
be paid for.

Some Continentals

☐ Roger Peyrefitte   **THE JEWS**   50p
Lovely Osmonde shocks her family because she wants to marry a
Jew – but as the witty author scarifyingly shows: if she can't marry
someone with Jewish blood . . . there may well be no-one left she
can marry.

☐ Robert Musil   **YOUNG TORLESS**   30p
A homosexual novel from one of Europe's great modern writers
about four cadets enmeshed in the machinery of a Teutonic military
academy. The systematic bullying that only too often degenerates
into torture is horrifying reading. 'I strongly recommend it' – *Punch*

☐ Jean-Paul Sartre   **INTIMACY**   30p
Ranges over the whole field of today's arid spirituality, from the
anguished conflict between 'love' and 'sex' to the feverish childhood
of a fascist rabble-rouser-to-be. A key book to modern life.

☐ Agnar Mykle   **LASSO ROUND**
                               THE MOON   30p
The multi-million-selling novel of Scandinavian youth and sex.

☐ Alberto Moravia   **COMMAND AND I**
                               WILL OBEY YOU   30p
Twenty-seven short-short razor-sharp stories by the world-famous
author of THE WOMAN OF ROME. 'One of the greatest living
writers, and this volume is a harsh, pungent, delicious pleasure' –
New Statesman

☐ Hermann Hesse   **DEMIAN**   30p
Hesse has become a modern 'cult' figure. DEMIAN, eerily mystical,
deals with the progress of a confused young man to some sort of
final enlightment – which is achieved on a hallucinatory World
War I battlefield in the novel's climactic last chapter. DEMIAN is
already in its fourth Panther Books edition.

Obtainable from all booksellers and newsagents. If you have
any difficulty please send purchase price plus 7p postage per
book to Panther Cash Sales, P.O. Box 11, Falmouth, Cornwall.

I enclose a cheque/postal order for titles ticked above plus 7p
a book to cover postage and packing.

Name...

Address...

....